Robert Neilson Stephens

The Continental Dragoon

A Love Story of Philipse Manor-House in 1778

Robert Neilson Stephens

The Continental Dragoon
A Love Story of Philipse Manor-House in 1778

ISBN/EAN: 9783744747691

Printed in Europe, USA, Canada, Australia, Japan

Cover: Foto ©Andreas Hilbeck / pixelio.de

More available books at **www.hansebooks.com**

THE

CONTINENTAL DRAGOON

A Love Story of Philipse Manor-House
in 1778

BY

ROBERT NEILSON STEPHENS

AUTHOR OF
"AN ENEMY TO THE KING"

Illustrated by

H. C. EDWARDS

"Love's born of a glance, I say"

BOSTON
L. C. PAGE AND COMPANY
(INCORPORATED)
1898

Entered at Stationer's Hall, London

FIFTH THOUSAND

Colonial Press:
Electrotyped and Printed by C. H. Simonds & Co.
Boston, U. S. A.

CONTENTS.

LIST OF ILLUSTRATIONS.

CONTINENTAL DRAGOON.

CHAPTER I.

THE RIDERS.

"I DARE say 'tis a wild, foolish, dangerous thing ; but I do it, nevertheless ! As for my reasons, they are the strongest. First, I wish to do it. Second, you've all opposed my doing it. So there's an end of the matter !"

It was, of course, a woman that spoke, — moreover, a young one.

And she added :

" Drat the wind ! Can't we ride faster ? 'Twill be dark before we reach the manor-house. Get along, Cato !"

She was one of three on horseback, who went northward on the Albany post-road late in the after-noon of a gray, chill, blowy day in November, in the war-scourged year 1778. Beside the girl rode a young gentleman, wrapped in a dark cloak. The third horse, which plodded a short distance in the rear, carried a small negro youth and two large portmanteaus. The three riders made a group that was, as far as could be seen from their view-point, alone on the highway.

There were reasons why such a group, on that road at that time, was an unusual sight, — reasons familiar to any one who is well informed in the history of the Revolution. Unfortunately, most good Americans are better acquainted with the French Revolution than with our own, know more about the state of affairs in Rome during the reign of Nero than about the condition of things in New York City during the British occupation, and compensate for their knowledge of Scotch-English border warfare in remote times by their ignorance of the border warfare that ravaged the vicinity of the island of Manhattan, for six years, little more than a century ago.

Our Revolutionary War had reached the respectable age of three and a half years. Lexington, Bunker Hill, Brooklyn, Harlem Heights, White Plains, Trenton, Princeton, the Brandywine, Germantown, Bennington, Saratoga, and Monmouth — not to mention events in the South and in Canada and on the water — had taken their place in history. The army of the King of England had successively occupied Boston, New York, and Philadelphia ; had been driven out of Boston by siege, and had left Philadelphia to return to the town more pivotal and nearer the sea, — New York. One British commander-in-chief had been recalled by the British ministry to explain why he had not crushed the rebellion, and one British major-general had surrendered an army, and was now back in England defending his course and pleading in Parliament the cause of the Americans, to whom he was still a prisoner on parole. Our Continental army — called Continental because, like the general Congress, it served the whole union of British-settled Colonies or States on this continent, and was thus distinguished from the militia, which served in each case its particular Colony or State only — had experienced both defeats and victories in encounters with the King's troops and his allies, German, Hessian, and American Tory. It had endured the winter at Valley Forge while the British had fed, drunk, gambled, danced, flirted, and wenched in Philadelphia. The French alliance had been sanctioned. Steuben, Lafayette, DeKalb, Pulaski, Kosciusko, Armand, and other Europeans, had taken service with us. One plot had been made in Congress and the army to supplant Washington in the chief command, and had failed. The treason of General Charles Lee had come to naught, — but was to wait for disclosure till many years after every person concerned should be graveyard dust. We had celebrated two anniversaries of the Fourth of July. The new free and independent States had organized local governments. The King's appointees still made a pretence of maintaining the royal provincial governments, but mostly abode under the protection of the King's troops in New York. There also many of those Americans in the North took refuge who distinctly professed loyalty to the King. New York was thus the chief lodging-place of all that embodied British sovereignty in America. Naturally the material tokens of British rule radiated from the town, covering all of the island of Manhattan, most of Long Island, and all of Staten Island, and retaining a clutch here and there on the mainland of New Jersey.

It was the present object of Washington to keep those visible signs of English authority penned up within this circle around New York. The Continental posts, therefore, formed a vast arc, extending from the interior of New Jersey through Southeastern New York State to Long Island Sound and into Connecticut. This had been the situation since midsummer of 1778. It was but a detachment from our main army that had coöperated with the French fleet in the futile attempt to dislodge a British force from Newport in August of that year.

The British commander-in-chief and most of the

superior officers had their quarters in the best residences of New York. That town was packed snugly into the southern angle of the island of Manhattan, like a gift in the toe of a Christmas stocking. Southward, some of its finest houses looked across the Battery to the bay. Northward the town extended little beyond the common fields, of which the City Hall Square of 1898 is a reduced survival. The island of Manhattan — with its hills, woods, swamps, ponds, brooks, roads, farms, sightly estates, gardens, and · orchards — was dotted with the cantonments and garrisoned forts of the British. The outposts were, largely, entrusted to bodies of Tory allies organized in this country. Thus was much of Long Island guarded by the three Loyalist battalions of General Oliver De Lancey, himself a native of New York. On Staten Island was quartered General Van Cortlandt Skinner's brigade of New Jersey Volunteers, a troop which seems to have had such difficulty in finding officers in its own State that it had to go to New York for many of them, — or was it that so many more rich New York Loyalists had to be provided with commissions than the New York Loyalist brigades required as officers?

But the most important British posts were those which guarded the northern entrance to the island of Manhattan, where it was separated from the mainland by Spuyten Duyvel Kill, flowing westward into the Hudson, and the Harlem, flowing southward into the East River. King's Bridge and the Farmers' Bridge, not far apart, joined the island to the main ; and just before the Revolution a traveller might have made his choice of these two bridges, whether he wished to take the Boston road or the road to Albany. In 1778 the British "barrier" was King's Bridge, the northern one of the two, the watch-house being the tavern at the mainland end of the bridge. Not only the bridge, but the Hudson, the Spuyten Duyvel, and the Harlem, as well, were commanded by British forts on the island of Manhattan. Yet there were defences still further out. On the mainland was a line of forts extending from the Hudson, first eastward, then southward, to the East River. Further north, between the Albany road and the Hudson, was a camp of German and Hessian allies, foot and horse. Northeast, on Valentine's Hill, were the Seventy-first Highlanders. Near the mainland bank of the Harlem were the quarters of various troops of dragoons, most of them American Tory corps with English commanders, but one, at least, native to the soil, not only in rank and file, but in officers also, — and with no less dash and daring than by Tarleton, Simcoe, and the rest, was King George III. served by Captain James De Lancey, of the county of West Chester, with his "cowboys," officially known as the West Chester Light Horse.

Thus the outer northern lines of the British were just above King's Bridge. The principal camp of the Americans was far to the north. Each army was affected by conditions that called for a wide space of territory between the two forces, between the outer rim of the British circle, and the inner face of the American arc. Of this space the portion that lay bounded on the west by the Hudson, on the southeast by Long Island Sound, and cut in two by the southward-flowing Bronx, was the most interesting.. It was called the Neutral Ground, and neutral it was in that it had the protection of neither side, while it was ravaged by both. Foraged by the two armies, under the approved rules of war, it underwent further a constant, irregular pillage by gangs of mounted rascals who claimed attachment, some to the British, some to the Americans, but were not owned by either. It was, too, overridden by the cavalry of both sides in attempts to surprise outposts, cut off supplies, and otherwise harass and sting. Unexpected forays by the rangers and dragoons from King's Bridge and the Harlem were reciprocated by sudden visitations of American horse and light infantry from the Greenburg Hills and thereabove. The Whig militia of the county also took a hand against British Tories and marauders. Of the residents, many Tories fled to New York, some Americans went to the interior of the country, but numbers of each party held their ground, at risk of personal harm as well as of robbery. Many of the best houses were, at different times during the war, occupied as quarters by officers of either side. Little was raised on the farms save what the farmers could immediately use or easily conceal. The Hudson was watched by British war-vessels, while the Americans on their side patrolled it with whale-boats, long and canoe-like, swift and elusive. For the drama of partisan warfare, Nature had provided, in lower West Chester County, — picturesquely hilly, beautifully wooded, pleasantly watered, bounded in part by the matchless Hudson and the peerless Sound, — a setting unsurpassed.

Thus was it that Miss Elizabeth Philipse, Major John Colden, and Miss Philipse's negro boy, Cuff, all riding northward on the Albany post-road, a few miles above King's Bridge, but still within territory patrolled daily by the King's troops, constituted, on that bleak November evening in 1778, a group unusual to the time and place.

'Twas a wettish wind, concerning which Miss Elizabeth expressed, in the imperative mood, her will that it be dratted, — a feminine wind, truly, as was clear from its unexpected flarings up and sudden calmings down, its illogical whiskings around and eccentric changes of direction. Now it swept down the slope from the east, as if it meant to bombard the travellers with all the brown leaves of the hillside. Now it assailed them from the north, as if to impede their journey ; now rushed on them from the rear as if it had come up from New York to speed them on their way ; now attacked them in the left flank, armed with a raw chill from the Hudson. It blew Miss Elizabeth's hair about and additionally reddened her cheeks. It caused the young Tory major to frown, for the protection of his eyes, and thus to look more and more unlike the happy man that Miss Elizabeth's accepted suitor ought to have appeared.

"I make no doubt I've brought on me the anger of your whole family by lending myself to this. And yet I am as much against it as they are!" So spake the major, in tones as glum as his looks.

"'Twas a choice, then, between their anger and mine," said Miss Elizabeth, serenely. "Don't think I wouldn't have come, even if you had refused your escort. I'd have made the trip alone with Cuff, that's all."

"I shall be blamed, none the less."

"Why? You couldn't have hindered me. If the excursion is as dangerous as they say it is, your company certainly does not add to my danger. It lessens it. So, as my safety is what they all clamor about, they ought to commend you for escorting me."

"If they were like ever to take that view, they would not all have refused you their own company."

"They refused because they neither supposed that I would come alone nor that Providence would send me an escort in the shape of a surly major on leave of absence from Staten Island! Come, Jack, you needn't tremble in dread of their wrath. By this time my amiable papa and my solicitous mamma and my anxious brothers and sisters are in such a state of mind about me that, when you return to-night and report I've been safely consigned to Aunt Sally's care, they'll fairly worship you as a messenger of good news. So be as cheerful as the wind and the cold will let you. We are almost there. It seems an age since we passed Van Cortlandt's."

Major Colden merely sighed and looked more dismal, as if knowing the futility of speech.

"There's the steeple!" presently cried the girl, looking ahead. "We'll be at the parsonage in ten minutes, and safe in the manor-house in five more. Do look relieved, Jack! The journey's end is in sight, and we haven't had sight of a soldier this side of King's Bridge, — except Van Wrumb's Hessians across Tippett's Vale, and they are friends. Br–r–r–r! I'll have Williams make a fire in every room in the manor-house!"

Now while these three rode in seeming security from the south towards the church, parsonage, country tavern, and great manor-house that constituted the village then called, sometimes Lower Philips-burgh and sometimes Younker's, that same hill-varied, forest-set, stream-divided place was being approached afar from the north by a company of mounted troops riding as if the devil was after them. It was not the devil, but another body of cavalry, riding at equal speed, though at a great distance behind. The three people from New York as yet neither saw nor heard anything of these horsemen dashing down from the north. Yet the major's spirits sank lower and lower, as if he had an omen of coming evil.

He was a handsome young man, Major John Colden, being not more than twenty-seven years old, and having the clearly outlined features best suited to that period of smooth-shaven faces. His dark eyes and his pensive expression were none the less effective for the white powder on his cued hair. A slightly petulant, uneasy look rather added to his countenance. He was of medium height and regular figure. He wore a civilian's cloak or outer coat over the uniform of his rank and corps, thus hiding also his sword and pistol. Other externals of his attire were riding-boots, gloves, and a three-cornered hat without a military cockade. He was mounted on a sorrel horse a little darker in hue than the animal ridden by Miss Elizabeth's black boy, Cuff, who wore the rich livery of the Philipses.

The steed of Miss Elizabeth was a slender black, sensitive and responsive to her slightest command — a fit mount for this, the most imperious, though not the oldest, daughter of Colonel Frederick Philipse, third lord, under the bygone royal régime, of the manor of Philipsburgh in the Province of New York. They gave classic names to quadrupeds in those days and Addison's tragedy was highly respected, so Elizabeth's scholarly father had christened this horse Cato. Howsoever the others who loved her regarded her present jaunt, no opposition was shown by Cato. Obedient now as ever, the animal bore her zealously forward, be it to danger or to what she would.

Elizabeth's resolve to revisit the manor hall on the Hudson, which had been left closed up in the steward's charge when the family had sought safety in their New York City residence in 1777, had sprung in part from a powerful longing for the country and in part from a dream which had reawakened strongly her love for the old house of her birth and of most of her girlhood. The peril of her resolve only increased her determination to carry it out. Her parents, brothers, and sisters stood aghast at the project, and refused in any way to countenance it. But there was no other will in the Philipse household able to cope with Elizabeth's. She held that the thing was most practicable and simple, inasmuch as the steward, with the aid of two servants, kept the deserted house in a state of habitation, and as her mother's sister, Miss Sarah Williams, was living with the widow Babcock in the parsonage of Lower Philipsburgh and could transfer her abode to the manor-house for the time of Elizabeth's stay. Major Colden, an unloved lover, — for Elizabeth, accepting marriage as one of the inevitables, yet declared that she could never love any man, love being admittedly a weakness, and she not a weak person, — was ever watchful for the opportunity of ingratiating himself with the superb girl, and so fearful of displeasing her that he dared not refuse to ride with her. He was less able even than her own family to combat her purpose. One day some one had asked him why, since she called him Jack, and he was on the road to thirty years, while she was yet in her teens, he did not call her Betty or Bess, as all other Elizabeths were called in those days. He meditated a moment, then replied, " I never heard any one, even in her own family, call her so. I can't imagine any one ever calling her by any more familiar name than Elizabeth."

Now it was not from her father that this regal young creature could have taken her resoluteness, though she may well have got from him some of the pride that went with it. There certainly must have been more pride than determination in Frederick Philipse, third lord of the manor, colonel in provincial militia before the Revolution, graduate of King's College, churchman, benefactor, gentleman of literary tastes ; amiable, courtly, and so fat that he and his handsome wife could not comfortably ride in the same coach at the same time.   But there was surely as much determination as pride in this gentleman's great-grandfather, Vrederyck Flypse, descendant of a line of viscounts and keepers of the deer forests of Bohemia, Protestant victim of religious persecution in his own land, immigrant to New Amsterdam about 1650, and soon afterward the richest merchant in the province, dealer with the Indians, ship-owner in the East and West India trade, importer of slaves, leader in provincial politics and government, founder of Sleepy Hollow Church, probably a secret trafficker with Captain Kidd and other pirates, and owner by purchase of the territory that was erected by royal charter of William and Mary into the lordship and manor of Philipsburgh.   The strength of will probably declined, while the pride throve, in transmission to Vrederyck's son, Philip, who sowed wild oats, and went to the Barbadoes for his health and married the daughter of the English governor of that island. Philip's son, Frederick, being born in a hot climate, and grandson of an English governor as well as of the great Flypse, would naturally have had great quantity of pride, whatever his stock of force, particularly as he became second lord of the manor at the lordly age of four.   And he could not easily have acquired humility in later life, as speaker of the provincial Assembly, Baron of the Exchequer, judge of the Supreme Court, or founder of St. John's Church, — towards which graceful edifice was the daughter of his son, the third lord, directing her horse this wintry autumn evening.   As for this third lord, he had been removed by the new Government to Connecticut for favoring the English rule, but, having received permission to go to New York for a short time, had evinced his fondness for the sweet and soft things of life by breaking his parole and staying in the city, under the British protection, thus risking his vast estate and showing himself a gentleman of anything but the courage now displayed by his daughter.

Elizabeth, therefore, must have derived her spirit, with a good measure of pride and a fair share (or more) of vanity, from her mother, though, thanks to that appreciation of personal comfort which comes with middle age, Madam Philipse's high-spiritedness would no longer have displayed itself in dangerous excursions, nor was it longer equal to a contest with the fresher energy of Elizabeth.   She was the daughter of Charles Williams, once naval officer of the port of New York, and his wife, who had been Miss Sarah Olivier.   Thus came Madam Philipse honestly by the description, "imperious woman of fashion," in which local history preserves her memory. She was a widow of twenty-four when Colonel Philipse married her, she having been bereaved two years before of her first husband, Mr. Anthony Rutgers, the lawyer. She liked display, and her husband indulged her inclination without stint, receiving in repayment a good nursery-full of what used, in the good old days, to be called pledges of affection. Being the daughter of a royal office-holding Englishman, how could she have helped holding her head mighty high on receiving her elevation to the ladyship of Philipsburgh, and who shall blame her daughter and namesake, now within a stone's throw of St. John's parsonage and in full sight of the tree-bowered manorial home of her fathers, for holding hers, which was younger, a trifle higher?

Not many high-held heads of this or any other day are or were finer than that of Elizabeth Philipse was in 1778, or are set on more graceful figures. For all her haughtiness, she was not a very large person, nor yet was she a small one. She was neither fragile nor too ample. Her carriage made her look taller than she was. She was of the brown-haired, blue-eyed type, but her eyes were not of unusual size or surpassing lucidity, being merely clear, honest, steady eyes, capable rather of fearless or disdainful attention than of swift flashes or coquettish glances. The precision with which her features were outlined did not lessen the interest that her face had from her pride, spirit, independence, and intelligence. She was, more-over, an active, healthy creature, and if she com-manded the dratting of the wind, it was not as much because she was chilled by it as because it blew her cloak and impeded her progress. In fine, she was a beauty; else this historian would never have taken the trouble of unearthing from many places and piecing together the details of this fateful incident, —for if any one supposes that the people of this narrative are mere fictions, he or she is radically in error. They lived and achieved, under the names they herein bear; were as actual as the places herein mentioned, —as any of the numerous patriotic Amer-icans who daily visit the genealogical shelves of the public libraries can easily learn, if they will spare sufficient time from the laudable task of hunting down their own ancestors. If this story is called a romance, that term is used here only as it is oft ap-plied to actual occurrences of a romantic character. So the Elizabeth Philipse who, before crossing the Neperan to approach the manor-house, stopped in front of the snug parsonage at the roadside and directed Cuff to knock at the door, was as real as was then the parsonage itself.

Presently a face appeared furtively at one of the up-stairs windows. The eyes thereof, having dwelt for an instant on the mounted party shivering in the road, opened wide in amazement, and a minute later, after a sound of key-turning and bolt-drawing, the door opened, and a good-looking lady appeared in the doorway, backed up by a servant and two pretty children who clung, half-curious, half-frightened, to the lady's skirts.

"Why, Miss Elizabeth! Is it possible —"

But Elizabeth cut the speech of the astonished lady short.

"Yes, my dear Mrs. Babcock, — and I know how dangerous, and all that! And, thank you, I'll not come in. I shall see you during the week. I'm going to the manor-house to stay awhile, and I wish my aunt to stay there with me, if you can spare her."

"Why, yes, — of course, — but — here comes your aunt."

"Why, Elizabeth, what in the world —."

She was a somewhat stately woman at first sight, was Elizabeth's mother's sister, Miss Sarah Williams; but on acquaintance soon conciliated and found to be not at all the formidable and haughty person she would have had people believe her; not too far gone in middle age, preserving, despite her spinsterhood, much of her bloom and many of those little round-nesses of contour which adorn but do not encumber.

"I haven't time to say what, aunt," broke in Elizabeth. "I want to get to the manor-house before it is night. You are to stay with me there a week. So put on a wrap and come over as soon as you can, to be in time for supper. I'll send a boy for you, if you like."

"Why, no, there's some one here will walk over with me, I dare say. But, la me, Elizabeth, — "

"Then I'll look for you in five minutes. Good night, Mrs. Babcock! I trust your little ones are well."

And she rode off, followed by Colden and Cuff, leaving the two women in the parsonage doorway to exchange what conjectures and what ejaculations of wonderment the circumstances might require.

Night was falling when the riders crossed the Neperan (then commonly known as the Saw Mill River) by the post-road bridge, and gazed more closely on the stone manor-house. Looking westward, from the main road, across the hedge and paling fence, they saw, first the vast lawn with its comely trees, then the long east front of the house, with its two little entrance-porches, the row of windows in each of its two stories, the dormer windows projecting from the sloping roof, the balustraded walk on the roof-top; at both ends the green and brown and yellow hints of what lay north of the house, between it and the forest, and west of the house, between it and the Hudson, — the box-hedged gardens, the terraces breaking the slope to the river, the deer paddock enclosed by high pickets, the great orchard. The Hudson was nearer to the house then than now, and its lofty further bank, rich with growth of wood and leaf, was the backing for the westward view. To the east, which the riders put behind them in facing the manor-house, were the hills of the interior.

"Not a sign of light from the house, and the shutters all closed, as if it were a tomb! It looks as cold and empty as one. I'll soon make it warm and live enough inside at least!" said Elizabeth, and turned westward from the highway into the short road that ran between the mansion and the north bank of the Neperan, by the grist-mill and the gate and the stables, down a picturesque descent to a landing where that stream entered the Hudson.

She proceeded towards the gate, where, being near the southeast corner of the house, one could see that the south front was to the east front as the base to the upright of a capital L turned backward; that the south front resembled the east in all but in being shorter and having a single porched entrance, which was in its middle.

As the party neared the gate, there arose far northward a sound of many horsemen approaching at a fast gallop. Elizabeth at once reined in, to listen. Major Colden and Cuff followed her example, both looking at her in apprehension. The galloping was on the Albany road, but presently deviated eastwardly, then decreased.

"They've turned up the road to Mile Square, whoever they are," said Elizabeth, and led the way on to the gate, which Cuff, dismounting, quickly opened, its fastening having been removed and not replaced. "Lead your horse to the door, Cuff. Then take off the portmanteaus and knock, and tie the horses to the post."

She rode up to the southern door in the east front, and was there assisted to dismount by the major, while Cuff followed in obedience. Colden, as the sound of the distant galloping grew fainter and fainter, showed more relief than he might have felt had he known that a second troop was soon to come speeding down in the track of the first.

Elizabeth, in haste to escape the wind, stepped into the little porch and stood impatiently before the dark, closed door of the house of her fathers.

CHAPTER II.

THE stone mansion before which the travellers stood, awaiting answer to Cuff's loud knock on the heavy mahogany door, had already acquired antiquity and memories. It was then, as to all south of the porch which now sheltered the three visitors, ninety-six years old, and as to the rest of the eastern front thirty-three, so that its newest part was twice the age of Elizabeth herself.

Her grandfather's grandfather, the first lord of the manor, built the southern portion in 1682, a date not far from that of the erection of his upper house, called Philipse Castle, at what is now Tarrytown, — but whether earlier or later, let the local historians dispute. This southern portion comprised the entire south front, its length running east and west, its width going back northward to, but not including, the large east entrance-hall, into which opened the southern door of the east front. The new part, attached to the original house as the upright to the short, broad base of the reversed L, was added by Elizabeth's grandfather, the second lord, in 1745. The addition, with the eastern section of the old part, was thereafter the most used portion, and the south front yielded in importance to the new east front. The two porched doors in the latter front matched each other, though the southern one gave entrance to the fine guests in silk and lace, ruffles and furbelows, who came up from New York and the other great mansions of the county to grace the frequent festivities of the Philipses; while the northern one led to the spacious kitchen where means were used to make the aforesaid guests feel that they had not arrived in vain.

The original house, rectangular as to its main part, had two gables, and, against its rear or northern length, a pent-roofed wing, and probably a veranda, the last covering the space later taken by the east entrance-hall. The main original building, on its first floor, had (and has) a wide entrance-hall in its middle, with one large parlor on each side. The second floor, reached by staircase from the lower hall, duplicated the first, there being a middle hall and two great square chambers. Overhead, there was plentiful further room beneath the gable roof. Under the western room of the first floor was the earlier kitchen, which, before 1745, served in relation to the guests who entered by the southern door exactly as thereafter the new kitchen served in relation to those entering by the eastern door,—

making them glad they had come, by horse or coach, over the long, bad, forest-bordered roads. Adjacent to the old kitchen was abundant cellarage for the stowing of many and diverse covetable things of the trading first lord's importation.

The Neperan joined the Hudson in the midst of wilderness, where Indians and deer abounded, when Vrederyck Flypse caused the old part of the stone mansion to grow out of the green hill slope in 1682. He planted a foundation two feet thick and thereupon raised walls whose thickness was twenty inches. He would have a residence wherein he might defy alike the savage elements, men and beasts. For the front end of his entrance-hall he imported a massive mahogany door made in 1681 in Holland, — a door in two parts, so that the upper half could be opened, while the lower half remained shut. The rear door of that hall was similarly made. Ponderous were the hinges and bolts, being ordinary blacksmith work. Solid were the panel mouldings. He brought Holland brick wherewith to trim the openings of doorways and windows. He laid the floor of his aforesaid kitchen with blue stone. The chimney breasts and hearthstones of his principal rooms were seven feet wide.

Here, in feudal fashion, with many servants and slaves to do his bidding, and tenants to render him dues, sometimes dwelt Vrederyck Flypse, with his second wife, Catherine Van Cortlandt, and the children left by his first wife, Margaret Hardenbrock; but sometimes some of the family lived in New York, and sometimes at the upper stone house, "Castle Philipse," by the Pocantico, near Sleepy Hollow Church, of this Flypse's founding. He built mills near both his country-houses, and from the saw-mill near the lower one did the Neperan receive the name of Saw Mill River. He died in 1702, in his seventy-seventh year, and the bones of him lie in Sleepy Hollow Church.

But even before the first lord went, did "associations" begin to attach to the old Dutch part of the mansion. Besides the leading families of the province, the traders, — Dutch and English, — and the men with whom he held counsel upon affairs temporal and spiritual, public and private, terrestrial and marine, he had for guests red Indians, and, there is every reason to believe, gentlemen who sailed the seas under what particular flag best promoted their immediate purposes, or under none at all. That old story never *would* down, to the effect that the adventurous Kidd levied not on the ships of Vrederyck Flypse. The little landing-place where Neperan joined Hudson, at which the Flypses stepped ashore when they came up from New York by sloop instead of by horse, was trodden surely by the feet of more than one eminent oceanic exponent of —

> " The good old rule, the simple plan,
>   That they should take who have the power
>   And they should keep who can."

A great merchant may have more than one way of doing business, and I would not undertake to account for every barrel and box that was unladen at that little landing.   Nor would I be surprised to encounter sometime, among the ghosts of Philipse Manor Hall, that of the immortal Kidd himself, seated at dead of night, across the table from the first lord of the manor, before a blazing log in the seven-foot fireplace, drinking liquor too good for the church-founding lord to have questioned whence it came; and leaving the next day without an introduction to the family.

This 1682 part of the house, in facing south, had the Albany road at its left, the Hudson at its right, and at its front the lane that ran by the Neperan, from the road to the river.   Thus was the house for sixty-three years.   When the first lord's grandson, Elizabeth's grandfather, in 1745 made the addition at the north, what was the east gable-end of the old house became part of the east front of the completed mansion.   The east rooms of the old house were thus the southeast rooms of the completed mansion, and, being common to both fronts, gained by the change of relation, becoming the principal parlor and the principal chamber.   The east parlor, entered on the west from the old hall, was entered on the north from the new hall; and the new hall was almost a duplicate of the old, but its ceiling decorations and the mahogany balustrade of its stairway were the more elaborate. This stairway, like its fellow in the old hall, ascended, with two turns, to a hall in the second story. Besides the new halls, the addition included, on the first floor, a large dining-room and the great kitchen; on the second floor, five sleeping-chambers, and, in the space beneath the roof-tree, dormitories for servants and slaves. Elizabeth's grandfather gave the house the balustrade that crowns its roof from its northern to its southern, and thence to its western end. He had the interior elaborately finished. The old part and its decorations were Dutch, but now things in the province were growing less Dutch and more English, — like the Philipse name and blood themselves, — and so the new embellishments were English. The second lord imported marble mantels from England, had the walls beautifully wainscoted, adorned the ceilings richly with arabesque work in wood. He laid out, in the best English fashion, a lawn between the eastern front and the Albany post-road. He it was who married Joanna, daughter of Governor Anthony Brockholst, of a very ancient family of Lancashire, England; and who left provision for the founding of St. John's Church, across

the Neperan from the manor-house, and for the
endowment of the glebe thereof.   And in his long
time the manor-house flourished and grew venerable
and multiplied its associations.   He had five children :
Frederick (Elizabeth's father), Philip, Susannah, Mary
(the beauty, wooed of Washington in 1756, 'tis said,
and later wed by Captain Roger Morris), and Margaret ; and, at this manor-house alone, white servants
thirty, and black servants twenty; and a numerous
tenantry, happy because in many cases the yearly
rent was but nominal, being three or four pounds or
a pair of hens or a day's work, — for the Philipses,
thanks to trade and to office-holding under the Crown,
and to the beneficent rule whereby money multiplies
itself, did not have to squeeze a living out of the
tillers of their land.   The lord of the manor held
court leet and baron at the house of a tenant, and
sometimes even inflicted capital punishment.

In 1751, the second lord followed his grandfather
to the family vault in Sleepy Hollow Church.   With
the accession of Elizabeth's father, then thirty-one
years old, began the splendid period of the mansion ;
then the panorama of which it was both witness and
setting wore its most diverse colors.   The old contest between English and French on this continent
was approaching its glorious climax.   Whether they
were French emissaries coming down from Quebec,
by the Hudson or by horse, or English and colonial

officers going up from New York in command of troops, they must needs stop and pay their respects to the lord of the manor of Philipsburgh, and drink his wine, and eat his venison, and flirt with his stunning sisters. Soldiers would go from New York by the post-road to Philipsburgh, and then embark at the little landing, to proceed up the Hudson, on the way to be scalped by the red allies of the French or mowed down by Montcalm's gunners before impregnable Ticonderoga. Many were the comings and goings of the scarlet coat and green. The Indian, too, was still sufficiently plentiful to contribute much to the environing picturesqueness. But, most of all, in those days, the mansion got its character from the festivities devised by its own inmates for the entertainment of the four hundred of that time.

For Elizabeth's mother, of the same given name, was "very fond of display," and in her day the family "lived showily." Her husband (who was usually called Colonel Philipse, from his title in the militia, and rarely if ever called lord) had the house refurnished. It was he who had the princely terraces made on the slope between the mansion and the Hudson, and who had new gardens laid out and adorned with tall avenues of box and rarest fruit-trees and shrubs. Doubtless his deer, in their picketed enclosure, were a sore temptation to the country marksmen who passed that way.   Lady, or Madam, or Mrs. Philipse, the colonel's wife, bedazzled the admiring inhabitants of West Chester County in many ways, but there is a difference between authorities as to whether it was she that used to drive four superb black horses over the bad roads of the county, or whether it was her mother-in-law, the second lord's wife.   Certainly it was the latter that was killed by a fall from a carriage, and certainly both had fine horses and magnificent coaches, and drove over bad roads, — for all roads were bad in those days, even in Europe, save those the Romans left.

Of all the gay and hospitable occasions that brought, through the mansion's wide doors, courtly gentlemen and high-and-mighty ladies, from their coaches, sleighs, horses, or Hudson sloops, perhaps none saw more feasting and richer display of ruffles and brocade than did the wedding of Mary Philipse and Captain Morris, seven years after the death of her father, and two after the marriage of her brother.   It was on the afternoon of Sunday, Jan. 15, 1758.   In the famous east parlor, which has had much mention and will have more in course of this narrative, was raised a crimson canopy emblazoned with the Philipse crest, — a crowned golden demi-lion rampant, upon a golden coronet. Though the weather was not severe, there was snow on the ground, and the guests began to drive up in sleighs, under the white trees, at two o'clock.   At three arrived the Rev. Henry Barclay, rector of Trinity, New York, and his assistant, Mr. Auchmuty. At half-past three the beauteous Mary (did so proud a heart-breaker blush, I wonder?) and the British captain stood under the crimson canopy and gold, and were united, "in the presence of a brilliant assembly," says the old county historian.' Miss Barclay, Miss Van Cortlandt, and Miss De Lancey were the bridesmaids, and the groomsmen were Mr. Heathcote (of the family of the lords of the manor of Scarsdale), Captain Kennedy (of Number One, Broadway), and Mr. Watts. No need to report here who were "among those present." The wedding did not occur yesterday, and the guests will not be offended at the omission of their names; but one of them was Acting Governor De Lancey. Colonel Philipse — wearing the ancestral gold chain and jewelled badge of the keepers of the deer forests of Bohemia — gave the bride away, and with her went a good portion of the earth's surface, and much money, jewelry, and plate.

After the wedding came the feast, and the guests — or most of them — stayed so late they were not sorry for the brilliant moonlight of the night that set in upon their feasting. And now the legend! In the midst of the feast, there appeared at the door of the banquet-hall a tall Indian, with a scarlet blanket close about him, and in solemn tones quoth he,

"Your possessions shall pass from you when the eagle shall despoil the lion of his mane." Thereupon he disappeared, of course, as suddenly as he had come, and the way in which historians have treated this legend shows how little do historians apply to their work the experiences of their daily lives, — such an experience, for instance, as that of ignoring some begging Irishwoman's request for "a few pennies in the Lord's name," and thereupon receiving a volley of hair-raising curses and baleful predictions. 'Tis easy to believe in the Indian and the prophecy of a passing of possessions, even though it was fulfilled; but the time-clause involving the eagle and the lion was doubtless added after the bird had despoiled the beast.

It was years and years afterward, and when and because the eagle had decided to attempt the said despoiling, that there was a change of times at Philipse Manor Hall. Meanwhile had young Frederick, and Maria, and Elizabeth, and their brothers and sisters arrived on the scene. What could one have expected of the ease-loving, beauty-loving, book-loving, luxury-loving, garden-loving, and wide-girthed lord of the manor — connected by descent, kinship, and marriage with royal office-holding — but Toryism? In fact, nobody did expect else of him, for though he tried in 1775 to conceal his sympathy with the cause of the King, the powers in revolt inferred it, and took measures to deter him from actively aiding the British forces. His removal to Hartford, his return to the manor-house, — where he was for awhile, in the fall of 1776, at the time of the battle of White Plains, — his memorable business trip to New York, and his parole-breaking continuance there, heralded the end of the old régime in Philipse Manor Hall. The historians say that at that time of Colonel Philipse's last stay at the hall, Washington quartered there for awhile, and occupied the great southwestern chamber. Doubtless Washington did occupy that chamber once upon a time, but his itinerary and other circumstances are against its having been immediately before or immediately after the battle of White Plains. Some of the American officers were there about the time. As for the colonel's family, it did not abandon the house until 1777. With the occasions when, during the first months of Revolutionary activity in the county, use was sought of the secret closets and the underground passage thoughtfully provided by the earlier Philipses in days of risk from Indians, fear of Frenchmen, and dealings with pirates, this history has naught to do.

In 1777, then, the family took a farewell view of the old house, and somewhat sadly, more resentfully, wended by familiar landmarks to New York, — to await there a joyous day of returning, when the

King's regiments should have scattered the rebels and hanged their leaders.   John Williams, steward of the manor, was left to take care of the house against that day, with one white housemaid, who was of kin to him, and one black slave, a man.   The outside shutters of the first story, the inside shutters above, were fastened tight; the bolts of the ponderous mahogany doors were strengthened, the stables and mills and outbuildings emptied and locked.   Much that was precious in the house went with the family and horses and servants to New York.   Yet be sure that proper means of subsistence for Williams and his two helpers were duly stowed away, for the faithful steward had to himself the discharge of that matter.

So wholesale a departure went with much bustle, and it was not till he returned from seeing the numerous party off, and found himself alone with the maid and the slave in the great entrance-hall, which a few minutes before had been noisy with voices, that Williams felt to the heart the sudden loneliness of the place.   The face of Molly, the maid, was white and ready for weeping, and there was a gravity on the chocolate visage of black Sam that gave the steward a distinctly tremulous moment. Perhaps he recalled the prediction of the Indian, and had a flash of second sight, and perceived that the third lord of the manor was to be the last.

Howbeit, he cleared his throat and set black' Sam to laying in fire-wood as for a siege, and Molly to righting the disorder caused by the exodus; betook himself cellarward, and from a hidden place drew forth a bottle of an old vintage, and comforted his solitude. He was a snug, honest, discreet man of forty, was the steward, slim but powerful, looking his office, besides knowing and fulfilling it.

But, as the months passed, he became used to the solitude, and the routine of life in the closed-up, memory-haunted old house took on a certain charm. The living was snug enough in what parts of the mansion the steward and his two servitors put to their own daily use. As for the other parts, the great dark rooms and entrance-halls, we may be sure that when the steward went the rounds, and especially after a visit to the wine-cellar, he found them not so empty, but peopled with the vague and shifting images of the many beings, young and old, who had filled the house with life in brighter days. Then, if ever, did noise of creaking stair or sound as of human breath, or, perchance, momentary vision of flitting face against the dark, betray the present ghost of some old-time habitué of the mansion.

When the raiding and foraging and marauding began in the county, the manor-house was not molested. The partisan warfare had not yet reached its magnitude. After the battle of White Plains in 1776, the British had retained New York City, while the main American army, leaving a small force above, had gone to New Jersey. Late in 1777, the British main army, leaving New York garrisoned, had departed to contest with the Americans for Philadelphia. Not until July, 1778, after Monmouth battle, did the British main army return to New York, and the American forces form the great arc, with their chief camp in upper West Chester County. Then was great increase of foray and pillage. The manor-house was of course exempt from harm at the hands of King's troops and Tory raiders, while it was protected from American regulars by Washington's policy against useless destruction, and from the marauding "Skinners" by its nearness to the British lines and by the solidity of its walls, doors, and shutters. Its gardens suffered, its picket fences and gate fastenings were tampered with, its orchards prematurely plucked. But its trees were spared by the British foragers, and the house itself was no longer in demand as officers' quarters, being too near King's Bridge for safe American occupancy, but not sufficiently near for British. Hessians and Tories, though, patrolled the near-by roads, and sometimes Continental troops camped in the neighboring hills. In 1778, the American Colonel Gist, whose corps was then at the foot of Boar Hill, north of the manor-house, was paying his court to the handsome widow Babcock, in the parsonage, when he was surprised by a force of yagers, rangers, and Loyalist light horse, and got away in the nick of time.[2] The parsonage, unlike the manor-house, was often visited by officers on their way hither and thither, but I will not say it was for this reason that Miss Sally Williams, the sister of Colonel Philipse's wife, preferred living in the parsonage with the Babcocks rather than in the great deserted mansion.

On a dark November afternoon, Williams had sent black Sam to the orchard for some winter apples, and the slave, after the fashion of his race, was taking his time over the errand. The shades of evening gathered while the steward was making his usual rounds within the mansion. Molly, whose housewifely instincts ever asserted themselves, had of her own accord made a dusting tour of the rooms and halls. She was on the first landing of the stairway in the east hall, just about to finish her task in the waning light admitted by the window over the landing and by the fanlight over the front door, when, as she applied her cloth to the mahogany balustrade, the door of the east parlor opened, and Williams came out of that dark apartment.

"Lord, Molly!" he said, a moment later, having started at suddenly beholding her. "I thought you were a ghost! It's time to get supper, I think,

from the look of the day outside.   I'll have to make
a light."

From a closet in the side of the staircase he took
a candle, flint, and tinder, talking the while to Molly,
as she rubbed the balusters.   Having produced a
tiny candle-flame that did not light up half the
hall, Williams started towards the dining-room, but
stopped at a distant sound of galloping horses,
which were evidently coming down the Albany road.
The steward and the maid exchanged conjectures as
to whether this meant a British patrol or "Rebel"
dragoons, "Skinners" or Hessian yagers, Highlanders, or Loyalist light horse ; and then observed
from the sound that the horses had turned aside
into the Mile Square road.

But now came a new sound of horses, and though
it was of only a few, and those walking, it gave
Williams quite a start, for the footfalls were manifestly approaching the mansion.   They as manifestly
stopped before that very h..l.   And then came a
sharp knock on the mahogany door.

"See who it is," whispered Molly.

Williams hesitated.   The knock was repeated.

"Who's there?" called out Williams.

There was an answer, but the words could not
be made out.

"Who?" repeated Williams.

This time the answer was clear enough.

"It's I, Williams! Don't keep me standing here in the wind all night."

"It's Miss Elizabeth!" cried Molly; and Williams, in a kind of daze of astonishment, hastily unlocked, unbolted, and threw open the door.

CHAPTER III.

THE SOUND OF GALLOPING.

A RUSH of wind came in from the outer gloom and almost blew out the candle. Williams held up his hand to protect the flame and stepped aside from before the doorway.

The wind was promptly followed by Elizabeth, who strode in with the air that a king might show on reëntering one of his palaces, still holding her whip in her gloved hand. Behind her came Colden, the picture of moody dejection. When Cuff had entered with the portmanteaus, Williams, seeing but three horses without, closed the door, locked it, and looked with inquiry and bewilderment at Elizabeth.

"Br–r–r–r!" she ejaculated. "Light up my chamber, Molly, and have a fire in it; then make some hot tea, and get me something to eat."

Elizabeth's impetuosity sent the open-mouthed maid flying up-stairs to execute the first part of the order, whereupon the mistress turned to the wondering steward.

"I've come to spend a week at the manor-house, Williams. Cuff, take those to my room."

The black boy, with the portmanteaus, followed in the way Molly had taken, but with less rapidity. By this time Williams had recovered somewhat from his surprise, and regained his voice and something of his stewardly manner.

"I scarcely expected any of the family out from New York these times, miss. There —"

"I suppose not!" Elizabeth broke in. "Have some one put away the horses, Williams, or they'll be shivering. It's mighty cold for the time of year."

"I'll go myself, ma'am. There's only black Sam, you know, and he isn't back from the orchard. I sent him to get some apples." And the steward set the candlestick on the newel post of the stairway, and started for the door.

"No, let Cuff go," said Elizabeth, sitting down on a settle that stood with its back to the side of the staircase. "You start a fire in the room next mine, for aunt Sally. She'll be over from the parsonage in a few minutes."

Williams thereupon departed in quest of the stable key, inwardly devoured by a mighty curiosity as to the wherefore of Elizabeth's presence here in the company of none but her affianced, and also the wherefore of that gentleman's manifest depression of spirits. His curiosity was not lessened when the major called after him:

"Tell Cuff he may feed my horse, but not take

the saddle off. I must ride back to New York as
soon as the beast is rested."

"Why," said Elizabeth to Colden, "you may stay
for a bite of supper."

"No, thank you! I am not hungry."

"A glass of wine, then," said the girl, quite heedless of his tone; "if there is any left in the house."

"No wine, I thank you!" Colden stood motionless, too far back in the hall to receive much light
from the feeble candle, like a shadowy statue of the
sulks.

"As you will!"

Whereupon Elizabeth, as if she had satisfied her
conscience regarding what was due from her in the
name of hospitality, rose, and opened the door to
the east parlor.

"Ugh! How dark and lonely the house is! No
wonder aunt Sally chose to live at the parsonage."
After one look into the dark apartment, she closed
the door. "Well, I'll warm up the place a bit.
Sorry you can't stay with us, major."

"It is only you who send me away," said Colden, dismally and reproachfully. "I could have got
longer leave of absence. You let me escort you
here, because no gentleman of your family will lend
himself to your reckless caprice. And then, having
no further present use for me, you send me about
my business!"

Elizabeth, preferring to pace the hall until her chamber should be heated, and her aunt should arrive, was striking her cloak with her riding-whip at each step; not that the cloak needed dusting, but as a method of releasing surplus energy.

"But I do have further present use for you," she said. "You are going back to New York to inform my dear timid parents and sisters and brothers that I've arrived here safe. They'll not sleep till you tell them so."

"One of your slaves might bear that news as well," quoth the major.

"Well, are you not forever calling yourself my slave? Besides, my devotion to King George won't let me weaken his forces by holding one of his officers from duty longer than need be."

But Colden was not to be cheered by pleasantry.

"What a man you are! So cross at my sending you back that you'll neither eat nor drink before going. Pray don't pout, Colden. 'Tis foolish!"

"I dare say! A man in love does many foolish things!"

The utterance of this great and universal truth had not time to receive comment from Elizabeth before Cuff reappeared, with the stable key; and at the same instant, a rather delicate, inoffensive knock was heard on the front door.

"That must be aunt Sally," said Elizabeth.

"Let her in, Cuff.   Then go and stable the horses. My poor Cato will freeze!"

It was indeed Miss Sarah Williams, and in a state of breathlessness.   She had been running, perhaps to escape the unseemly embraces of the wind, which had taken great liberties with her skirts, — liberties no less shocking because of the darkness of the evening; for though De la Rochefoucauld has settled it that man's alleged courage takes a vacation when darkness deprives it of possible witnesses, no one will accuse an elderly maiden's modesty of a like eclipse.

" My dear child, what could have induced you — " were her first words to Elizabeth ; but her attention was at that point distracted by seeing Cuff, outside the threshold, about to pull the door shut.   " Don't close the door yet, boy.   Some one is coming."

Cuff thereupon started on his task of stabling the three horses, leaving the door open.   The flame of the candle on the newel post was blown this way and that by the in-rushing wind.

" It's old Mr. Valentine," explained Miss Sally to Elizabeth.   " He offered to show me over from the parsonage, where he happened to be calling, so I didn't wait for Mrs. Babcock's boy — "

" You found Mr. Valentine pleasanter company, I suppose, aunty, dear," put in Elizabeth, who spared neither age nor dignity.   " He's a widower again, isn't he ?"

Miss Sally blushed most becomingly. Her plump cheeks looked none the worse for this modest suffusion.

"Fie, child! He's eighty years old. Though, to be sure, the attentions of a man of his experience and judgment aren't to be considered lightly."

Those were the days when well-bred people could — and often did, naturally and without effort — improvise grammatical sentences of more than twelve words, in the course of ordinary, every-day talk.

"We started from the parsonage together," went on Miss Sally, "but I was so impatient I got ahead. He doesn't walk as briskly as he did twenty years ago."

Yet briskly enough for his years did the octogenarian walk in through the little pillared portico a moment later. Such deliberation as his movements had might as well have been the mark of a proper self-esteem as the effect of age. He was a slender but wiry-looking old gentleman, was Matthias Valentine, of Valentine's Hill; in appearance a credit to the better class of countrymen of his time. His white hair was tied in a cue, as if he were himself a landowner instead of only a manorial tenant. Yet no common tenant was he. His father, a dragoon in the French service, had come down from Canada and settled on Philipse Manor, and Matthias had been proprietor of Valentine's Hill, renting from the Philipses in earlier days than any one could remember. His grandsons now occupied the Hill, and the old man was in the full enjoyment of the leisure he had won. His rather sharp countenance, lighted by honest gray eyes, was a mixture of good-humor, childlike ingenuousness, and innocent jocosity. The neatness of his hair, his carefully shaven face, and the whole condition of his brown cloth coat and breeches and worsted stockings, denoted a fastidiousness rarely at any time, and particularly in the good (or bad) old days, to be found in common with rustic life and old age. Did some of the dandyism of the French dragoon survive in the old Philipsburgh farmer?

He carried a walking-stick in one hand, a lighted lantern in the other. After bowing to the people in the hall, he set down his lantern, closed the door and bolted it, then took up his lantern, blew out the flame thereof, and set it down again.

"Whew!" he puffed, after his exertion. "Windy night, Miss Elizabeth! Windy night, Major Colden! Winter's going to set in airly this year. There ain't been sich a frosty November since '64, when the river was froze over as fur down as Spuyten Duyvel."

There was in the old man's high-pitched voice a good deal of the squeak, but little of the quaver, of senility.

"You'll stay to supper, I hope, Mr. Valentine."

From Elizabeth this was a sufficient exhibition of graciousness. She then turned her back on the two men and began to tell her aunt of her arrangements.

"Thankee, ma'am," said old Valentine, whose sight did not immediately acquaint him, in the dim candle-light, with Elizabeth's change of front ; wherefore he continued, placidly addressing her back : "I wouldn't mind a glass and a pipe with friend Williams afore trudging back to the Hill."

He then walked over to the disconsolate Colden, and, with a very gay-doggish expression, remarked in an undertone :

"Fine pair o' girls yonder, major?"

He had known Colden from the time of the latter's first boyhood visits to the manor, and could venture a little familiarity.

"Girls?" blurted the major, startled out of his meditations.

The old country beau chuckled.

"We all know what's betwixt you and the niece. How about the aunt and me taking a lesson from you two, eh?"

Even the gloomy officer could not restrain a momentary smile.

"What, Mr. Valentine? Do you seriously think of marrying?"

"Why not? I've been married afore, hain't I? What's to hinder?"

"Why, there's the matter of age." Colden rather enjoyed being inconsiderate of people's feelings.

"Oh, the lady is not so old," said the octogenarian, placidly, casting a judicial, but approving look at the commanding figure of Miss Sally.

Then, as he had been for a considerable time on his legs, having walked over from the Hill to the parsonage that afternoon, and as at best his knees bent when he stood, he sat down on the settle by the staircase.

Miss Sally, though she knew it useless to protest further against Elizabeth's caprice, nevertheless felt it her duty to do so, especially as Major Colden would probably carry to the family a report of her attitude towards that caprice.

"Did you ever hear of such rashness, major? A young girl like Elizabeth coming out here in time of war, when this neutral ground between the lines is overridden and foraged to death, and deluged with blood by friend as well as foe? La me! I can't understand her, if she *is* my sister's child."

"Why, aunt Sally, *you* stay out here through it all," said Elizabeth, not as much to depreciate the dangers as to give her aunt an opportunity of posing as a very courageous person.

Miss Sally promptly accepted the opportunity.

"Oh," said she, with a mien of heroic self-sacrifice, "I couldn't let poor Grace Babcock stay at the parsonage with nobody but her children ; besides I'm not Colonel Philipse's daughter, and who cares whether I'm loyal to the King or not ? But a girl like you isn't made for the dangers and privations we've had to put up with out here since the King's troops have occupied New York, and Washington's rebel army has held the country above. I'm surprised the family let her come, or that you'd countenance it by coming with her, major."

"We all opposed it," said Colden, with a sigh. "But — you know Elizabeth !"

"Yes," said Elizabeth herself with cheerful nonchalance, "Elizabeth always has her way. I was hungry for a sight of the place, and the more the old house is in danger, the more I love it. I'm here for a week, and that ends it. The place doesn't seem to have suffered any. They haven't even quartered troops here."

"Not since the American officers stayed here in the fall o' '76," put in old Mr. Valentine, from the settle. "I reckon you'll be safe enough here, Miss Elizabeth."

"Of course I shall. Why, our troops patrol all this part of the country, Lord Cathcart told us at King's Bridge, and *we* have naught to fear from them."

"No, the British foragers won't dare treat Phil-

ipse Manor-house as they do the homes of some of
their loyal friends," said Miss Sally, who was no less
proud of her relationship with the Philipses, because
it was by marriage and not by blood. "But the hor-
rible "Skinners," who don't spare even the farms of
their fellow rebels — "

"Bah!" said Elizabeth. "The scum of the earth!
Williams has weapons here, and with him and the
servants I'll defend the place against all the rebel
cut-throats in the county."

The major thought to make a last desperate
attempt to dissuade Elizabeth from remaining.

"That's all well enough," said he; "but there are
the rebel regulars, the dragoons. They'll be raiding
down to our very lines, one of these days, if only in
retaliation. You know how Lord Cornwallis's party
under General Grey, over in Jersey, the other night,
killed a lot of Baylor's cavalry, — Mrs. Washington's
Light Horse, they called the troop. And the Hessians made a great foray on the rebel families this
side the river."

"Ay," chirped old Valentine; "but the American
Colonel Butler, and their Major Lee, of Virginia, fell
on the Hessian yagers 'tween Dobbs's Ferry and
Tarrytown, and killed ever so many of 'em, — and I
wasn't sorry for that, neither!"

"Oho!" said Colden, "you belong to the opposition."

"Oh, I'm neither here nor there," replied the old man. "But they say that there Major Lee, of Virginia, is the gallantest soldier in Washington's army. He'd lead his men against the powers of Satan if Washington gave the word. Light Horse Harry, they call him, — and a fine dashing troop o' light horse he commands."

"No more dashing, I'll wager, than some of ours," said Elizabeth, whose mood for the moment permitted her to talk with reason and moderation; "not even counting the Germans. And as for leaders, what do you say to Simcoe, of the Queen's Rangers, or Emmerick, or Tarleton, or" — turning to Colden — "your cousin James De Lancey, of this county, major?"

The major, notwithstanding his Toryism, did not enter with enthusiasm into Elizabeth's admiration for these brave young cavalry leaders. Staten Island and East New Jersey had not offered him as great opportunities for distinction as they had had. It was, therefore, Miss Sally who next spoke.

"Well, Heaven knows there are enough on either side to devastate the land and rob us of comfort and peace. One wakes in the middle of the night, at the clatter of horses riding by like the wind, and wonders whether it's friend or foe, and trembles till they're out of hearing, for fear the door is to be broken in or the house fired. And the sound of shots in the night, and the distant glare of flames when some poor farmer's home is burned over his head!"

"Ay," added Mr. Valentine, "and all the cattle and crops go to the foragers, so it's no use raising any more than you can hide away for your own larder."

Elizabeth was beginning to be bored, and saw nothing to gain from a continuation of these recitals. Doubtless, by this time, her room was lighted and warm.   So, thoughtless of Colden, she mounted the first step of the stairway, and said :

"I have no doubt Williams has contrived to hide away enough provisions for *our* use.   So *I* sha'n't suffer from hunger, and as for Lee's Light Horse, I defy them and all other rebels.   Come, aunt Sally!"

She had ascended as far as to the fourth step of the stairway, and Miss Sally was about to follow, when there was heard, above the wind's moaning, another sound of galloping horses.   Like the previous similar sound, it came from the north.

Elizabeth stopped and stood on the fourth step. Miss Sally raised her finger to bid silence.   Colden's attitude became one of anxious attention, while he dropped his hat on the settle and drew his cloak close about him, so that it concealed his uniform, sword, and pistol.   The galloping continued.

When time came for it to turn off eastward, as it

would do should the riders take the road to Mile Square, it did not so. Instead, as the sound unmistakably indicated, it came on down the post-road.

"Hessians, perhaps!" Miss Sally whispered.

"Or De Lancey's Cowboys," said Valentine, but not in a whisper.

Elizabeth cast a sharp look at the old man, as if to show disapproval of his use of the Whigs' nickname for De Lancey's troop. But the octogenarian did not quail.

"They're riding towards the manor-house," he added, a moment later.

"Let us hope they're friends," said Colden, in a tone low and slightly unsteady.

Elizabeth disdained to whisper.

"Maybe it is Lee's Light Horse," she said, in her usual voice, but ironically, addressing Valentine. "In that case we should tremble for our lives, I suppose."

"Whoever they are, they've stopped before the house!" said Miss Sally, in quite a tremble.

There was a noise of horses pawing and snorting outside, of directions being given rapidly, and of two or three horses leaving the main band for another part of the grounds. Then was heard a quick, firm step on the porch floor, and in the same instant a sharp, loud knock on the door.

No one in the hall moved; all looked at Elizabeth.

"A very valiant knock!" said she, with more

irony. "It certainly *must* be Lee's Light Horse. Will you please open the door, Colden?"

"What?" ejaculated Colden.

"Certainly," said Elizabeth, turning on the stairway, so as to face the door; "to show we're not afraid."

Jack Colden looked at her a moment demurringly, then went to the door, undid the fastenings, and threw it open, keeping his cloak close about him and immediately stepping back into the shadow.

A handsome young officer strode in, as if 'twere a mighty gust of wind that sent him. He wore a uniform of blue with red facings, — a uniform that had seen service, — was booted and spurred, without greatcoat or cloak. A large pistol was in his belt, and his left hand rested on the hilt of a sword. He swept past Colden, not seeing him; came to a stop in the centre of the hall, and looked rapidly around from face to face.

"Your servant, ladies and gentlemen!" he said, with a swift bow and a flourish of his dragoon's hat. His eye rested on Elizabeth.

"Who are you?" she demanded, coldly and imperiously, from the fourth step.

"I'm Captain Peyton, of Lee's Light Horse," said he.

CHAPTER IV.

THE CONTINENTAL DRAGOON.

THE Peytons of Virginia were descended from a younger son of the Peytons of Pelham, England, of which family was Sir Edward Peyton, of Pelham, knight and baronet. Sir Edward's relative, the first American Peyton, settled in Westmoreland County. Within one generation the family had spread to Stafford County, and within another to Loudoun County also. Thus it befell that there was a Mr. Craven Peyton, of Loudoun County, justice of the peace, vestryman, and chief warden of Shelburne Parish. He was the father of nine sons and two daughters. One of the sons was Harry.

This Harry grew up longing to be a soldier. Military glory was his ambition, as it had been Washington's; but not as a mere provincial would he be satisfied to excel. He would have a place as a regular officer, in an army of the first importance, on the fields of Europe. Before the Revolution, Americans were, like all colonials, very loyal to their English King. Therefore would Harry Peyton be content with naught less than a King's commission in the King's army.

His father, glad to be guided in choosing a future for one of so many sons, sent Harry to London in 1770, to see something of life, and so managed matters, through his English relations, that the boy was in 1772, at the age of nineteen, the possessor, by purchase, of an ensign's commission. He was soon sent to do garrison duty in Ireland, being enrolled with the Sixty-third Regiment of Foot.

He had lived gaily enough during his two years in London, occupying lodgings, being patronized by his relations, seeing enough of society, card-tables, drums, routs, plays, prize-fights, and other diversions. He had made visits in the country and showed what he had learned in Virginia about cock-fighting, fox-hunting and shooting, and had taken lessons from London fencing-masters. A young gentleman from Virginia, if well off and " well connected," could have a fine time in London in those days; and Harry Peyton had it.

But he could never forget that he was a colonial. If he were treated by his English associates as an equal, or even at times with a particular consideration, there was always a kind of implication that he was an exception among colonials. Other colonial youths were similarly treated, and some of these were glad to be held as exceptions, and even joined in the derision of the colonials who were not. For these Harry Peyton had a mighty disgust and detestation. He did not enjoy receiving as Harry Peyton a tolerance and kindness that would have been denied him as merely an American. And he sometimes could not avoid seeing that, even as Harry Peyton, he was regarded as compensating, by certain attractive qualities in the nature of amiability and sincerity, for occasional exhibitions of what the English rated as social impropriety and bad taste. Often, at the English lofty derision of colonials, at the English air of self-evident superiority, the English pretence of politely concealed shock or pain or offence at some infringement of a purely superficial conduct-code of their own arbitrary fabrication, he ground his teeth in silence; for in one respect, he had as good manners as the English had then, or have now, — when in Rome he did not resent or deride what the Romans did. He began to think that the lot of a self-respecting American among the English, even if he were himself made an exception of and well dealt with, was not the most enviable one. And, after he joined the army, he thought this more and more every day. But he would show them what a colonial could rise to! Yet that would prove nothing for his countrymen, as he would always, on his meritorious side, be deemed an exception.

His military ambition, however, predominated, and he had no thought of leaving the King's service.

The disagreement between the King and the

American Colonies grew, from "a cloud no bigger than a man's hand," to something larger. But Harry heard little of it, and that entirely from the English point of view. He received but three or four letters a year from his own people, and the time had not come for his own people to write much more than bare facts. They were chary of opinions. Harry supposed that the new discontent in the Colonies, after the repeal of the Stamp Act and the withdrawal of the two regiments from Boston Town to Castle William, was but that of the perpetually restless, the habitual fomenters, the notoriety-seeking agitators, the mob, whose circumstances could not be made worse and might be improved by disturbances. Now the Americans, from being a subject of no interest to English people, a subject discussed only when some rare circumstance brought it up, became more talked of. Sometimes, when Americans were blamed for opposing taxes to support soldiery used for their own protection, Harry said that the Americans could protect themselves; that the English, in wresting Canada from the French, had sought rather English prestige and dominion than security for the colonials; that the flourishing of the Colonies was despite English neglect, not because of English fostering; that if the English had solicitude for America, it was for America as a market for their own trade. Thereupon his fellow officers would either laugh him out, as if he were too ignorant to be argued with, or freeze him out, as if he had committed some grave outrage on decorum. And Harry would rage inwardly, comparing his own ignorance and indecorousness with the knowledge and courtesy exemplified in the assertion of Doctor Johnson, when that great but narrow Englishman said, in 1769, of Americans, "Sir, they are a race of convicts, and ought to be thankful for anything we allow them short of hanging."

There came to Harry, now and then, scraps of vague talk of uneasiness in Boston Town, whose port the British Parliament had closed, to punish the Yankees for riotously destroying tea on which there was a tax; of the concentration there of British troops from Halifax, Quebec, New York, the Jerseys, and other North American posts. But there was not, in Harry's little world of Irish garrison life, the slightest expectation of actual rebellion or even of a momentous local tumult in the American Colonies.

Imagine, therefore, his feelings when, one morning late in March in 1775, he was told that, within a month's time, the Sixty-third, and other regiments, would embark at Cork for either Boston or New York!

There could not be a new French or Spanish invasion. As for the Indians, never again would

British regulars be sent against them. Was it, then, Harry's own countrymen that his regiment was going to fight?

His comrades inferred the cause of his long face, and laughed. He would have no more fighting to do in America against the Americans than he had to do in Ireland against the Irish, or than an English officer in an English barrack town had to do against the English. The reinforcements were being sent only to overawe the lawless element. The mere sight of these reinforcements would obviate any occasion for their use. The regiment would merely do garrison duty in America instead of in Ireland or elsewhere.

He had none to advise or enlighten him. What was there for him to do but sail with his regiment, awaiting disclosures or occurrences to guide? What misgivings he had, he kept to himself, though once on the voyage, as he looked from the rocking transport towards the west, he confided to Lieutenant Dalrymple his opinion that 'twas damned bad luck sent *his* regiment to America, of all places.

When he landed in Boston, June 12th, he found, as he had expected, that the town was full of soldiers, encamped on the common and quartered elsewhere; but also, as he had not expected, that the troops were virtually confined to the town, which was fortified at the Neck; that the last

time they had marched into the country, through
Lexington to Concord, they had marched back
again at a much faster gait, and left many score
dead and wounded on the way; and that a host
of New Englanders in arms were surrounding Boston! The news of April 19th had not reached Europe until after Harry had sailed, nor had it met
his regiment on the ocean. When he heard it now,
he could only become more grave and uneasy. But
the British officers were scornful of their clodhop-
per besiegers. In due time this rabble should be
scattered like chaff. But was it a mere rabble?
Certainly. Were not the best people in Boston
loyal to the King's government? Some of them,
yes. But, as Harry went around with open eyes
and ears, eager for information, he found that many
of them were with the "rabble." News was easy
to be had. The citizens were allowed to pass the
barrier on the Neck, if they did not carry arms or
ammunition, and there was no strict discipline in
the camp of New Englanders. Therefore Harry
soon learned how Doctor Warren stood, and the
Adamses, and Mr. John Hancock; and that a Congress, representing all the Colonies, was now sitting
at Philadelphia, for the second time; and that in
the Congress his own Virginia was served by such
gentlemen as Mr. Richard Henry Lee, Mr. Patrick
Henry, Mr. Thomas Jefferson, and Colonel Wash-

ington. And the Virginians had shown as ready and firm a mind for revolt against the King's measures as the New Englanders had. Here, for once, the sympathies of trading Puritan and fox-hunting Virginian were one. Moreover, a Yankee was a fellow American, and, after five years of contact with English self-esteem, Harry warmed at the sight of a New Englander as he never would have done before he had left Virginia.

But it did not conduce to peace of mind, in his case, to be convinced that the colonial remonstrance was neither local nor of the rabble. The more general and respectable it was, the more embarrassing was his own situation. Would it really come to war? With ill-concealed anxiety, he sought the opinion of this person and that.

On the fourth day after his arrival, he went into a tavern in King Street with Lieutenant Massay, of the Thirty-fifth, Ensign Charleton, of the Fifth, and another young officer, and, while they were drinking, heard a loyalist tell what one Parker, leader of the Lexington rebels, said to his men on Lexington Common, on the morning of April 19th, when the King's troops came in sight.

"'Stand your ground,' says he. 'Don't fire till you're fired on, but if they mean to have a war, let it begin here!'"

"And it began there!" said Harry.

The English officers stared at him, and laughed.

"Ay, 'twas the Yankee idea of war," said one of them. "Run for a stone wall, and, when the enemy's back is turned, blaze away. I'd like to see a million of the clodhoppers compelled to stand up and face a line of grenadiers."

"Ay, gimme ten companies of grenadiers," cried one, who had doubtless heard of General Gage's celebrated boast, "and I'll go from one end of the damned country to the other, and drive 'em to their holes like foxes. Only 'tis better sport chasing handsome foxes in England than ill-dressed poltroons in Bumpkin-land."

"They're not all poltroons," said Harry, repressing his feelings the more easily through long practice. "Some of them fought in the French war. There's Putnam, and Pomeroy, and Ward. I heard Lieutenant-Colonel Abercrombie, of the Twenty-second, say yesterday that Putnam —"

"Cowards every one of 'em," broke in another. "Cowards and louts. A lady told me t'other day there ain't in all America a man whose coat sets in close at the back, except he's of the loyal party. Cowards and louts!"

"Look here, damn you!" cried Peyton. "I want you to know I'm American born, and my people are American, and I don't know whether they are of the loyal party or not!"

"Oh, now, that's the worst of you Americans, — always will get personal! Of course, there are exceptions."

"Then there are exceptions enough to make a rule themselves," said Harry. "I'm tired hearing you call these people cowards before you've had a chance to see what they are. And you needn't wait for that, for I can tell you now they're not!"

"Well, well, perhaps not, — to you. Doubtless they're very dreadful, — to you. You don't seem to relish facing 'em, that's a fact! You'll be resigning your commission one o' these days, I dare say, if it comes to blows with these terrible heroes!"

Harry saw everybody in the room looking at him with a grin.

"By the Lord," said he, "maybe I shall!" and stalked hotly out of the place.

His wrath increased as he walked. He noticed now, more than before, the confident, arrogant air of the redcoats who promenaded the streets; how they leered at the women, and made the citizens who passed turn out of the way. Forthwith, he went to his quarters, and wrote his resignation.

When the ink was dry he folded up the document and put it in the pocket of his uniform coat. Then that last tavern speech recurred to him. "If I resign now," he thought, "they'll suppose it's because I really am afraid of fighting, not because the rebels are my countrymen." So he lapsed into a state of indecision, — a state resembling apathy, a half-dazed condition, a semi-somnolent waiting for events. But he kept his letter of resignation in his coat.

At dawn the next morning, Saturday, June 17th, he was awakened by the booming of guns. He was soon up and out. It was a beautiful day. People were on the eminences and roofs, looking northward, across the mouth of the Charles, towards Charlestown and the hill beyond. On that hill were seen rough earthworks, six feet high, which had not been there the day before. The booming guns were those of the British man-of-war *Lively*, firing from the river at the new earthworks. Hence the earthworks were the doing of the rebels, having been raised during the night. Presently the *Lively* ceased its fire, but soon there was more booming, this time not only from the men-of-war, but also from the battery on Copp's Hill in Boston. After awhile Harry saw, from where he stood with many others on Beacon Hill, some of the rebels emerge from one part of the earthworks, as if to go away. One of these was knocked over by a cannon-ball. His comrades dragged his body behind the earthen wall. By and by a tall, strong-looking man appeared on top of the parapet, and walked leisurely along, apparently giving directions. Harry heard from a citizen, who had a field-glass, the words, " Prescott, of Pepperell."

Other men were now visible on the parapet, superintending the workers behind.   And now the booming of the guns was answered by disrespectful cheers from those same unseen workers.

The morning grew hot.   Harry heard that General Gage had called a council of war at the Province House ; that Generals Howe, Clinton, Burgoyne,[3] — these three having arrived in Boston about three weeks before Harry had, — Pigott, Grant, and the rest were now there in consultation.   At length there was the half-expected tumult of drum and bugle; and Harry was summoned to obey, with his comrades, the order to parade.   There was now much noise of officers galloping about, dragoons riding from their quarters, and rattling of gun-carriages.   The booming from the batteries and vessels increased.

At half-past eleven Harry found himself — for he was scarcely master of his acts that morning, his will having taken refuge in a kind of dormancy — on parade with two companies of his regiment, and he noticed in a dim way that other companies near were from other different regiments, all being supplied with ammunition, blankets, and provisions.   When the sun was directly overhead and at its hottest, the order to march was given, and soon he was bearing the colors through the streets of Boston.   The roar of the cannon now became deafening.   Harry knew not whether the rebels were returning it from their hill works across the water or not. In time the troops reached the wharf. Barges were in waiting, and field-pieces were being moved into some of them. He could see now that all the firing was from the King's vessels and batteries. Mechanically he followed Lieutenant Dalrymple into a barge, which soon filled up with troops. The other barges were speedily brilliant with scarlet coats and glistening bayonets. Not far away the river was covered with smoke, through which flashed the fire of the belching artillery. A blue flag was waved from General Howe's barge, and the fleet moved across the river towards the hill where the rebels waited silently behind their piles of earth.

At one o'clock, Harry followed Lieutenant Dalrymple out of the barge to the northern shore of the river, at a point northeast of Charlestown village and east of the Yankees' hill. There was no molestation from the rebels. The firing from the vessels and batteries protected the hillside and shore. The troops were promptly formed in three lines. Harry's place was in the left of the front line. Then there was long waiting. The barges went back to the Boston side. Was General Howe, who had command of the movements, sending for more troops? Many of the soldiers ate of their stock of provisions. Harry, in a kind of dream, looked westward up the hill towards

the silent Yankee redoubt.   It faced south, west,
and east.   The line of its eastern side was continued northward by a breastwork, and still beyond
this, down the northern hillside to another river,
ran a straggling rail fence, which was thatched
with fresh-cut hay.   What were the men doing behind those defences?   What were they saying and
thinking?

The barges came back across the Charles from
Boston, with more troops, but these were disem-
barked some distance southwest, nearer Charlestown.
General Howe now made a short speech to the troops
first landed.   Then some flank guards were sent out
and some cannon wheeled forward.   The companies of
the front line, with one of which was Harry, were
now ordered to form into files and move straight
ahead.   They were to constitute the right wing of
the attacking force, and to be led by General Howe
himself.   The four regiments composing the two rear
lines moved forward and leftward, to form, with the
troops newly landed, the left wing, which was to be
under General Pigott.   The cannonading from the
river and from Boston continued.

The companies with which was Harry advanced
slowly, having to pass through high grass, over stone
fences, under a roasting sun.   These companies were
moving towards the hay-thatched rail fence that strag-
gled down the hillside from the breastwork north of

the redoubt. Harry had a vague sense that the left
wing was ascending the southeastern side of the hill,
towards the redoubt, at the same time. His eye
caught the view at either side. Long files of scarlet
coats, steel bayonets, grenadiers' tall caps. He looked
ahead. The stretch of green, grassy hillside, the
hay-covered rail fence looking like a hedge-row, the
rude breastwork, the blue sky. Suddenly there came
from the rail fence the belching of field-pieces. Two
grenadiers fell at the right of Harry. One moaned,
the other was silent. Harry, shocked into a sense
that war was begun between his King and his
people, instantly resolved to strike no blow that
day against his people. But this was no time for
leaving the ranks. Mechanically he marched on.

Heads appeared over the fence-rail, guns were
rested on it, and there came from it some irregular
flashes of musketry. Then Harry saw a man moving
his head and arms, as if shouting and gesticulating.
The musket flashes ceased. Harry did not know it
then, but the man was Putnam, and he was commanding the Yankees to reserve their fire. The
British files were now ordered to deploy into line,
and fire. They did so as they advanced, firing
in machine-like unison, as if on parade, but aiming
high. Nearer and nearer, as Harry went forward,
rose the fence ahead and the breastwork on the hill
towards the left. Why did not the Yankees fire?

Were they, indeed, paralyzed with fear at sight of the lines of the King's grenadiers?

All at once blazed forth the answer, — such a volley of musketry, at close range, as British grenadiers had not faced before. Down went officers and men, in twos and threes and rows. Great gaps were cut in the scarlet lines. The broken columns returned the volley, but there came another. Harry found himself in the midst of quivering, writhing, yelling death. The British who were left, — startled, amazed, — turned and fled. As mechanically as he had come up, did Harry go back in the common movement. General Howe showed astonishment. The left wing, too, had been hurled back, down the hill, by death-dealing volleys. The rabble had held their rude works against the King's choice troops. Never had as many officers been killed or wounded in a single charge. There had not been such mowing down at Fontenoy or Montmorenci. These unmilitary Yankees actually aimed when they fired, each at some particular mark! Harry had heard them cheering, and had thought they were about to pursue the King's troops; they had evidently been ordered back.

The troops re-formed by the shore. Orders came for another assault. Back again went Harry with the right wing, bearing the colors as before. He had secretly an exquisite heart-quickening elation at the success of his countrymen. If they should win the day, and hold this hill, and drive the King's troops from Boston! He knew, at last, on which side his heart was.

There was more play of artillery during this second charge. Harry could see, too, that the village of Charlestown was on fire, sending flames, sparks, and smoke far towards the sky. It was not as easy to go to the charge this time, there were so many dead bodies in the way. But the soldiers stepped over them, and maintained the straightness of their lines. Again it seemed as if the rebels would never fire. Again, when the King's troops were but a few rods from them, came that flaming, low-aimed discharge. But the troops marched on, in the face of it, till the very officers who urged them forward fell before it; then they wavered, turned, and ran. Harry's joy, as he went with them, increased, and his hopes mounted. The left wing, too, had been thrown back a second time.

There was a long wait, and the generals were seen consulting. At last a third charge was ordered. This time the greater part of the right wing was led up the hill against the breastwork. With this part was Harry. One more volley from the rebel defences met the King's troops. They wavered slightly, then sprang forward, ready for another. But another came not. The rebels' ammunition was giving out. Harry's heart fell. The British forced the breast-work, carrying him along. He found himself at the northern end of the redoubt. Some privates lifted him to the parapet; he and a sergeant mounted at the same time, and leaped together into the redoubt. They saw Lieutenant Richardson, of the Royal Irish Regiment, appear on the southern parapet, give a shout of triumph, and fall dead from a Yankee musket-ball. A whole rank that followed him was served likewise, but others surged over the parapet in their places. The rebels were defending mainly the southern parapet. Many were retreating by the rear passageway. Harry saw that the King's troops had won the redoubt. He took his resolution. He threw the colors to the sergeant, pulled off his coat, handed it to the same sergeant, shouting into the man's ear, "Give it to the colonel, with the letter in the pocket;" picked up a dead man's musket, and ran to the aid of a tall, powerful rebel who was parrying with a sword the bayonets of three British privates. The tramp of the retreating rebels, invading British, and hand-to-hand fighters raised a blinding dust. Harry and the tall American, gaining a breathing moment, strode together with long steps, guarding their flank and rear, to the passageway and out of it; and then fought their course between two divi-

"GIVE IT TO THE COLONEL.'"

sions of British, which had turned the outer corners of the redoubt. There was no firing here, so closely mingled were British and rebels, the former too exhausted to use forcibly their bayonets. So Harry retreated, beside the tall man, with the rebels. A British cheer behind him told the result of the day; but Harry cared little. His mind was at ease; he was on the right side at last.

Thus did young Mr. Peyton serve on both sides in the same battle, being with each in the time of its defeat, striking no blow against his country, yet deserting not the King's army till the moment of its victory. His act was indeed desertion, desertion to the enemy, and in time of action; for, though his resignation was written, it was not only unaccepted, but even undelivered. Thus did he render himself liable, under the laws of war, to an ignominious death should he ever fall into the hands of the King's troops.

During the flight to Cambridge, Harry was separated from the tall man with whom he had come from the redoubt, but soon saw him again, this time directing the retreat, and learned that he was Colonel Prescott, of Pepperell. Some of the rebels discussed Harry freely in his own hearing, inferring from his attire that he was of the British, and wondering why he was not a prisoner. Harry asked to be taken to the commander, and at Cambridge a coatless, bareheaded captain led him to General Ward, of the Massachusetts force. That veteran militiaman heard his story, gave it credit, and, with no thought that he might be a spy, invited him to remain at the camp as a volunteer. Harry obtained a suit of blue clothes, and quartered in one of the Harvard College buildings. In a few days news came that the Congress at Philadelphia had resolved to organize a Continental army, of which the New England force at Cambridge was to be the present nucleus; that a general-in-chief would soon arrive to take command, and that the general-in-chief appointed was a Virginian, — Colonel Washington. Harry was jubilant.

Early in July the new general arrived, and Harry paid his respects to him in the house of the college president. General Washington advised the boy to send another letter of resignation, then to go home and join the troops that his own State would soon be raising. On hearing Harry's story, Washington had given a momentary smile and a look at Major-General Charles Lee, who had but recently published his resignation of his half-pay as a retired British officer, and who did not know yet whether that resignation would be accepted or himself considered a deserter.

Peyton sent a new letter of resignation to Boston, then procured a horse, and started to ride to Virginia. Six days later he was in New York. In a coffee-house where he was dining, he struck up an acquaintance with three young gentlemen of the city, and told his name and story. One of the three — a dark-eyed man — thereupon changed manner and said he had no time for a rascally turncoat. Harry, in hot resentment, replied that he would teach a damned Tory some manners. So the four went out of the town to Nicholas Bayard's woods, where, after a few passes with rapiers, the dark-eyed gentleman was disarmed, and admitted, with no good grace, that Harry was the better fencer. Harry left New York that afternoon, having learned that his antagonist was Mr. John Colden, son of the post-master of New York. His grandfather had been lieutenant-governor.

Harry had for some time thought he would prefer the cavalry, and he was determined, if possible, to gratify that preference in entering the military service of his own country. On arriving home he found his people strongly sympathizing with the revolt. But it was not until June, 1776, that Virginia raised a troop of horse. On the 18th of that month Harry was commissioned a cornet thereof. After some service he found himself, March 31, 1777, cornet in the First Continental Dragoons. The next fall, in a skirmish after the battle of Brandywine, he was recognized by British officers as the former ensign of the Sixty-third. In the following spring, thanks to his activity during the British occupation of Philadelphia, he was made captain-lieutenant in Harry Lee's battalion of light dragoons. After the battle of Monmouth he was promoted, July 2, 1778, to the rank of captain. In the early fall of that year he was busy in partisan warfare between the lines of the two armies.

And thus it came that he was pursuing a troop of Hessians down the New York and Albany post-road on a certain cold November evening. Eager on the chase, he was resolved to come up with them if it could be, though he should have to ride within gunshot of King's Bridge itself. Suddenly his horse gave out. He had the saddle taken from the dead animal and given to one of his men to bear while he himself mounted in front of a sergeant, for he was loath to spare a man. Approaching Philipse Manor-house, the party saw a boy leading horses into a stable. Captain Peyton ordered some of his men to patrol the road, and with the rest he went on to the manor-house lawn.

Here he gave further directions, dismounted, knocked at the door, and was admitted to the hall where were Miss Elizabeth Philipse, Major Colden, Miss Sally Williams, and old Matthias Valentine; and, on Elizabeth's demand, announced his name and rank.

CHAPTER V.

THANKS to the dimness, to his uniform, and to his
swift entrance, Peyton had not been recognized by
Major Colden until he had given his name. That
name had on the major the effect of an apparition,
and he stepped back into the dark corner of the hall,
drawing his cloak yet closer about him. This alarm
and movement were not noticed by the others, as
Peyton was the object of every gaze but his own,
which was fixed on Elizabeth.

"What do you want?" her voice rang out, while
she frowned from her place on the staircase, in cold
resentment. Her aunt, meanwhile, made the new-
comer a tremulous curtsey.

"I want to see the person in charge of this house,
and I want a horse," replied Peyton, with more
promptitude than gentleness, yet with strict civility.
Elizabeth's manner would have nettled even a colder
man.

Elizabeth did not keep him waiting for an answer.

"I am at present mistress of this house, and I am
neither selling horses nor giving them!"

Peyton stared up at her in wonderment.

The candle-flame struggled against the wind, turning this way and that, and made the vague shadows of the people and of the slender balusters dance on floor and wall. From without came the sound of Peyton's horses pawing, and of his men speaking to one another in low tones.

"Your pardon, madam," said Peyton, "but a horse I must have. The service I am on permits no delay —"

"I doubt not!" broke in Elizabeth. "The Hessians are probably chasing you."

"On the contrary, I am chasing the Hessians. At Boar Hill, yonder, my horse gave out. 'Tis important my troops lose no time. Passing here, we saw horses being led into your stable. I ordered one of my men to take the best of your beasts, and put my saddle on it, — and he is now doing so."

"How dare you, sir!" and Elizabeth came quickly to the foot of the stairs, a picture of regal, flaming wrath.

"Why, madam," said Peyton, "'tis for the service of the army. I require the horse, and I have come here to pay for it —"

"It is not for sale —"

"That makes no difference. You know the custom of war."

"The custom of robbery!" cried Elizabeth.

Captain Peyton reddened.

"Robbery is not the custom of Harry Lee's dragoons, madam," said he, "whatever be the practice of the wretched 'Skinners' or of De Lancey's Tory Cowboys. I shall pay you as you choose, — with a receipt to present at the quartermaster's office, or with Continental bills."

"Continental rubbish!"

And, indeed, Elizabeth was not far from the truth in the appellation so contemptuously hurled.

"You prefer that, do you?" said Peyton, unruffled; whereupon he took from within his waistcoat a long, thick pocketbook, and from that a number of bills; which must have been for high amounts, for he rapidly counted out only a score or two of them, repocketing the rest, and at that time, thereabouts, "a rat in shape of a horse," as Washington himself had complained a month before, was "not to be bought for less than £200."⁺ Peyton handed her the bills he had counted out. "There's a fair price, then," said he; "allowing for depreciation. The current rate is five to one, — I allow six."

Elizabeth looked disdainfully at the proffered bills, and made no move to take them.

"Pah!" she cried. "I wouldn't touch your wretched Continental trash. I wouldn't let one of my black women put her hair up in it. Money, do you call it? I wouldn't give a shilling of the King for a houseful of it."

"I beg your pardon," said Peyton, cheerfully. "Since July in '76 there has been no king in America. I leave the bills, madam." He laid them on the newel post, beside the candlestick. "'Tis all I can do, and more than many a man would do, seeing that Colonel Philipse, the owner of this place, is no friend to the American cause, and may fairly be levied on as an enemy —"

"Colonel Philipse is my father!"

"Then I'm glad I've been punctilious in the matter," said Peyton, but without any increase of deference. "Egad, I think I've been as scrupulous as the commander-in-chief himself!"

"The commander-in-chief!" echoed Elizabeth. "Sir Henry Clinton pays in gold."

"I meant *our* commander-in-chief," with a suavity most irritating.

"Mr. Washington!" said Elizabeth, scornfully, with a slight emphasis on the "Mr."

"His Excellency, General Washington." Peyton spoke as one would in gently correcting a child who was impolite. Then he added, "I think the horse is now ready; so I bid you good evening!"

And he strode towards the door.

Elizabeth was now fully awake to the certainty that one of the horses would indeed be taken. At

Peyton's movement she ran to the door, reaching it before he did, and looked out. What she saw, transformed her into a very fury.

"Oh, this outrage!" she cried, facing about and addressing those in the hall. "It is my Cato they are leading out! My Cato! Under my very eyes! I forbid it! He shall not go! Where are Cuff and the servants? Why don't they prevent? And you, Jack?"

She turned to Colden for the first time since Peyton's arrival.

"My troop would make short work of any who interfered, madam," said Peyton, warningly, still looking at Elizabeth only.

"Oh, that I should have to endure this!" she said. "Oh, if I had but a company of soldiers at my back, you dog of a rebel!"

And she paced the hall in a great passion. Passing the newel post, she noticed the Continental bills. She took these up, violently tore them across, and threw the pieces about the hall, as one tosses corn about a chicken-yard.

Major Colden had been having a most uncomfortable five minutes. As a Tory officer, he was in close peril of being made prisoner by this Continental captain and the latter's troop outside, and this peril was none the less since he had so adversely criticised Peyton in the talk which had led to the duel in

Bayard's woods. He had not put himself on friendly terms with Peyton after that affair. There was still no reason for any other feeling towards him, on Peyton's part, than resentment. Now Jack Colden had no relish for imprisonment at the hands of the despised rebels. Moreover, he had no wish that Elizabeth should learn of his former defeat by Peyton. He had kept the meeting in Bayard's woods a secret, thanks to Peyton's having quitted New York immediately after it, and to the relation of dependence in which the two only witnesses stood to him. Thus it was that he had remained well out of view during Elizabeth's sharp interview with Peyton, being unwilling alike to be known as a Tory officer, and to be recognized by Peyton. His civilian's cloak hid his uniform and weapons; the dimness of the candle-light screened his face.

But matters had reached a point where he could not, without appearing a coward, refrain longer from taking a hand. He stepped forward from the dark remoteness.

"Sir," said he to Peyton, politely, "I know the custom of war. But since a horse must be taken, you will find one of mine in the stable. Will you not take it instead of this lady's?"

Peyton had been scrutinizing Colden's features.

"Mr. Colden, if I remember," he said, when the major had finished.

"You remember right," said Colden, with a bow, concealing behind a not too well assumed quietude what inward tremors the situation caused him.

"And you are doubtless now an officer in some Tory corps?" said Peyton, quickly.

"No, sir, I am neutral," replied Colden, rather huskily, with an instant's glance of warning at Elizabeth.

"Gad!" said Peyton, with a smile, still closely surveying the major. "From your sentiments the time I met you in New York in '75, I should have thought you'd take up arms for the King."

"That was before the Declaration of Independence," said Colden, in a tone scarcely more than audible. "I have modified my opinions."

"They were strong enough then," Peyton went on. "You remember how you upheld them with a rapier in Bayard's woods?"

"I remember," said Colden, faintly, first reddening, then taking on a pale and sickly look, as if a prey to hidden chagrin and rage.

It seemed as if his tormentor intended to torture him interminably. Peyton, who knew that one of his men would come for him as soon as the horse should be saddled and bridled, remained facing the unhappy major, wearing that frank half-smile which, from the triumphant to the crestfallen, seems so insolent and is so maddening.

"I've often thought," said Peyton, "I deserved small credit for getting the better of you that day. I had taken lessons from London fencing-masters." (Consider that the woman whom Colden loved was looking on, and that this was all news to her, and imagine how he raged beneath the outer calmness he had, for safety's sake, to wear.) "'Twas no hard thing to disarm you, and I'm not sorry you're neutral now. For if you wore British or Tory uniform, 'twould be my duty to put you again at disadvantage, by taking you prisoner."

The face of one of Peyton's men now appeared in the doorway. Peyton nodded to him, then continued to address the major.

"As for your request, my traps are now on the other horse, and there is not time to change. I must ride at once."

He stepped quickly to the door, and on the threshold turned to bow.

Then cried Elizabeth:

"May you ride to your destruction, for your impudence, you bandit!"

"Thank you, madam! I shall ride where I must! Farewell! My horse is waiting."

And in an instant he was gone, having closed the door after him with a bang.

"*His* horse! The highwayman!" quoth Elizabeth.

"Give the gentleman his due," said Miss Sally, in a way both mollified and mollifying. "He paid for it with those." She indicated the strewn fragments of the Continental bills on the floor.

"Forward! Get up!"

It was the voice of Captain Peyton outside. The horses were heard riding away from the lawn.

Elizabeth opened the door and looked out. Her aunt accompanied her. Old Valentine gazed with a sagely deploring expression at the torn-up bills on the floor. Colden stood where he had been, lest by some chance the enemy might return and discover his relief from straint.

"Oh," cried Elizabeth, at the door, as the light horsemen filed out the gate and up the branch road towards the highway, "to see the miserable rebel mounted on my Cato!"

"He looks well on him," said her aunt.

It was a brief flow of light from the fresh-risen moon, between wind-driven clouds, that enabled Miss Sally to make this observation.

"Looks well! The tatterdemalion!" And Elizabeth came from the door, as if loathing further sight of him.

But Miss Sally continued to look after the riders, as their dark forms were borne rapidly towards the post-road. "Nay, I think he is quite handsome."

"Pah! You think every man is handsome!" said the niece, curtly.

Miss Sally turned from the door, quite shocked.

"Why, Elizabeth, you know I'm the least susceptible of women!"

Old Mr. Valentine nodded sadly, as much as to say, "I know that, all too well!"

As the racing clouds now rushed over the moon, and the horsemen's figures, having become more and more blurred, were lost in the blackness, Miss Sally closed and bolted the door. The horses were faintly heard coming to a halt, at about the junction of the branch road with the highway, then moving on again rapidly, not further towards the south, as might have been expected, but back northward, and finally towards the east. Meanwhile Elizabeth stood in the hall, her rage none the less that its object was no longer present to have it wreaked on him. Such hate, such passionate craving for revenge, had never theretofore been awakened in her. And when she realized the unlikelihood of any opportunity for satisfaction, she was exasperated to the limit of self-control.

"If you had only had some troops here!" she said to Colden.

"I know it! May the rascal perish for finding me at such a disadvantage! 'Twas my choice between denying my colors and becoming his prisoner."

This brought back to Elizabeth's mind the talk

between Colden and Peyton, which her feelings had for the time driven from her thoughts. But now a natural curiosity asserted itself.

"So you knew the fellow before?"

"I met him in '75," said Colden, blurting awkwardly into the explanation that he knew had to be made, though little was his stomach for it. "He was passing through New York from Boston to his home in Virginia, after he had deserted from the King's army —"

"Deserted?" Elizabeth opened wide her eyes.

Colden briefly outlined, as far as was desirable, what he knew of Peyton's story.

It was Miss Sally who then said:

"And he disarmed you in a duel?"

"He had practised under London fencing-masters, as he but now admitted," replied Colden, grumpily. "He made no secret of his desertion; and in a coffee-house discussion I said it was a dastardly act. So we — fought. Since then I've met officers of the regiment he left. Such a thing was never known before, — the desertion of an officer of the Sixty-third, — and General Grant, its colonel, has the word of Sir Henry Clinton that this fellow shall hang if they ever catch him."

"Then I hope my horse will carry him into their hands!" said Elizabeth, heartily. "My poor Cato! I shall never see him again!"

"We may get him back some day," said Colden, for want of aught better to say.

"If you can do that, John Colden, and have this rebel hanged who dared treat me so —" Elizabeth paused, and her look dwelt on the major's face.

"Well?"

"Then I think I shall almost be really in love with you!"

But Colden sighed. "A rare promise from one's betrothed!"

"Heavens, Jack!" said Elizabeth, now diverted from the thought of her horse. "Don't I do the best I can to love you? I'm sure I come as near loving you as loving anybody. What more can I do than that, and promising my hand? Don't look dismal, major, I pray, — and now make haste back to New York."

"How can I go and leave you exposed to the chance of another visit from some troop of rebels?" pleaded Colden, in a kind of peevish despair, taking up his hat from the settle.

"Oh, that fellow showed no disposition to injure *me!*" she answered, reassuringly. "Trust me to take care of myself."

"But promise that if there's any sign of danger, you will fly to New York."

"That will depend on the circumstances. I may be safer in this house than on the road."

"Then, at least, you will have guns fired, and also send a man to one of our outposts for help?" There was no pretence in the young man's solicitude. Such a bride as Elizabeth Philipse was not to be found every day. The thought of losing her was poignant misery to him.

"To which one?" she asked. "The Hessian camp by Tippett's Brook, or the Highlanders', at Valentine's Hill?"

"No," said Colden, meditating. "Those may be withdrawn if the weather is bad. Send to the barrier at King's Bridge, — but if your man meets one of our patrols or pickets on the way, so much the better. Good-by! I shall see your father to-night, and then rejoin my regiment on Staten Island."

He took her hand, bent over it, and kissed it.

"Be careful you don't fall in with those rebel dragoons," said Elizabeth, lightly, as his lips dwelt on her fingers.

"No danger of that," put in old Valentine, from the settle, for the moment ceasing to chew an imaginary cud. "They took the road to Mile Square." The octogenarian's hearing was better than his sight.

"I shall notify our officers below that this rebel force is out," said Colden, "and our dragoons may cut it off somewhere. Farewell, then! I shall return for you in a week."

"In a week," repeated Elizabeth, indifferently.

He kissed her hand again, bowed to Miss Sally, and hastened from the hall, closing the door behind him. Once outside, he made his way to the stables, where he knew that Cuff, not having returned to Elizabeth, must still be.

"It's little reward you give that gentleman's devotion, Elizabeth," said Miss Sally, when he had gone.

"Why, am I not going to give him myself? Come, aunty, don't preach on that old topic. My parents wish me to be married to Jack Colden, and I have consented, being an obedient child, — in some things."

"More obedient to your own whims than to anything else," was Miss Sally's comment.

The sound of Colden's horse departing brought to the amiable aunt the thought of a previous departure.

"That fine young rebel captain!" said she. "If our troops take him they'll hang him! Gracious! As if there were so many handsome young men that any could be spared! Why can't they hang the old and ugly ones instead?"

Mr. Valentine suspended his chewing long enough to bestow on Miss Sally a look of vague suspicion.

The door, which had not been locked or bolted after Colden's going, was suddenly flung open to admit Cuff. The negro boy had been thrown by the dragoons' visit into an almost comatose condition of fright, from which the orders of Colden had but now sufficiently restored him to enable his venturing out of the stable. He now stood trembling in fear of Elizabeth's reproof, stammering out a wild protestation of his inability to save the horse by force, and of his inefficacious attempts to save him by prayer.

Elizabeth cut him short with the remark, intended rather for her own satisfaction than for aught else, that one thing was to be hoped, — the chance of war might pay back the impertinent rebel who had stolen the horse. She then gave orders that the hall and the east parlor be lighted up.

"For the proper reception," she added to her aunt, "of the next handsome rebel captain who may condescend to honor us with a visit. Mr. Valentine, wait in the parlor till supper is ready. I'll have a fire made there. Come, aunt Sally, we'll discuss over a cup of tea the charms of your pretty rebel captain and his agreeable way of relieving ladies of their favorite horses. I'll warrant he'll look handsomer than ever, on the gallows, when our soldiers catch him."

And she went blithely up the stairs, which at the first landing turned rightward to a second landing, and thence rightward again to the upper hall. The darkness was interrupted by a narrow stream of light from a slightly open doorway in the north side of this upper hall. This was the doorway to her own room, and when she crossed the threshold she saw a bright blaze in the fireplace, lights in a candelabrum, cups and saucers on a table, and Molly bringing in a steaming teapot from the next room, which, being northward, was nearer the kitchen stairs. This next room, too, was lighted up. Solid wooden shutters, inside the windows of both chambers, kept the light from being seen without, and the wind from being felt within.

As Elizabeth was looking around her room, smiling affectionately on its many well-remembered and long-neglected objects, there was a sudden distant detonation. Molly looked up inquiringly, but Elizabeth directed her to place the tea things, find fresh candles, if any were left in the house, and help Cuff put them on the chandelier in the lower hall, and then get supper. As Molly left the room, Miss Sally entered it.

"Elizabeth! Oh, child! There's firing beyond Locust Hill. It's on the Mile Square road, Mr. Valentine says, — cavalry pistols and rangers' muskets."

"Mr. Valentine has a fine ear."

"He says the rebel light horse must have met the Hessians! There 'tis again!"

"Sit down, aunt, and have a dish of tea. Ah—h!"

This is comfortable! Delicious! Let them kill one another as they please, beyond Locust Hill; let the wind race up the Hudson and the Albany road as it likes, — we're snugly housed!"

Williams, who had, from the upper hall, safely overheard Captain Peyton's intrusion, and had not seen occasion for his own interference, now came in from the next room, which he had been making ready for Miss Sally, and received Elizabeth's orders concerning the east parlor.

Meanwhile, what of Harry Peyton and his troop?

Riding up the little tree-lined road towards the highway, they saw dark forms of other riders standing at the point of junction. These were the men whom Peyton had directed to patrol the road. They now told him that, by the account of a belated farmer whom they had halted, the Hessians had turned from the highway into the Mile Square road. Peyton immediately led his men to that road. Thus, as old Valentine said, that part of the highway between the manor-house and King's Bridge remained clear of these rebel dragoons, and Major Colden stood in no danger of meeting them on his return to New York. The major, nevertheless, did not spare his horse as he pursued his lonely way through the windy darkness. When he arrived at King's Bridge he was glad to give his horse another rest, and to accept an invitation to a bottle and a game in the tavern where the British commanding officer was quartered.

The Hessians had not gone far on the Mile Square road, when their leader called a halt and consulted with his subordinate officer. They were now near Mile Square, where the Tory captain, James De Lancey, kept a recruiting station all the year round, and Valentine's Hill, where there was a regiment of Highlanders. Their own security was thus assured, but they might do more than come off in safety, — they might strike a parting blow at their pursuers. A plan was quickly formed. A messenger was despatched to Mile Square to request a small reinforcement. The troop then turned back towards the highway, having planned for either one of two possibilities. The first was that the rebel dragoons, not thinking the Hessians had turned into the Mile Square road, would ride on down the highway. In that case, the Hessians would follow them, having become in their turn the pursuers, and would fall upon their rear. The noise of firearms would alarm the Hessian camp by Tippett's Brook, below, and the rebels would thus be caught between two forces. The second possibility was that the Americans would follow into the Mile Square road. When the sound of their horses soon told that this was the reality, the Hessians promptly prepared to meet it.

The force divided into two parts. The foremost

blocked the road, near a turning, so as to remain unseen by the approaching rebels until almost the moment of collision. The second force stayed some rods behind the first, forming in two lines, one along each side of the road. As to each force, some were armed with sabres and cavalry pistols, but most, being mounted yagers of Van Wrumb's battalion, with rifles.

As for the little detachment of Lee's Light Horse that was now galloping along the Mile Square road, under Harry Peyton's command, the arms were mainly broadswords and pistols, but some of the men had rifles or light muskets.

The troop went forward at a gallop against the wind, there being just sufficient light for keen eyes to make out the road ahead. Harry Peyton was inwardly deploring the loss of time at Philipse Manor-house, and fearing that the prey would reach its covert, when suddenly the moon appeared in a cloud-rift, the troops passed a turn in the road, and there stood a line of Hessians barring the way.

Ere Peyton could give an order, came one loud, flaming, whistling discharge from that living barrier. Harry's horse — Elizabeth Philipse's Cato — reared, as did others of his troop. Some of the men came to a quick stop, others were borne forward by the impetus of their former speed, but soon reined in for orders. No man fell, though one groaned, and two cursed.

Harry got his horse under control, drew his broadsword with his right hand, his pistol with his left, — which held also the rein, — and ordered his men to charge, to fire at the moment of contact, then to cut, slash, and club.   So the little troop, the well and the wounded alike, dashed forward.

But the line of Hessians, as soon as they had fired, turned and fled, passing between the two lines of the second force, and stopping at some further distance to reform and reload.   The second force, being thus cleared by the first, wheeled quickly into the road, and formed a second barrier against Peyton's oncoming troop.

Peyton's men, intoxicated by the powder-smell that filled their nostrils as they passed through the smoke of the Hessians' first volley, bore down on this second barrier with furious force.   They were the best riders in the world, and many a one of them held his broadsword aloft in one hand, his pistol raised in the other, the rein loose on his horse's neck; while those with long-barrelled weapons aimed them on the gallop.

The Hessians and Peyton's foremost men fired at the same moment.   The Hessians had not time to turn and flee, for the Americans, unchecked by this second greeting of fire, came on at headlong speed. "At 'em, boys!" yelled Peyton, discharging his pistol at a tall yager, who fell sidewise from his horse with a fierce German oath. The light horse men dashed between the Hessians' steeds, and there was hewing and hacking.

A Hessian officer struck with a sabre at Peyton's left arm, but only knocked the pistol from his hand. Peyton then found himself threatened on the right by a trooper, and slashed at him with broadsword. The blow went home, but the sword's end became entangled somehow with the breast bones of the victim. A yager, thinking to deprive Peyton of the sword, brought down a musket-butt heavily on it. But Peyton's grip was firm, and the sword snapped in two, the hilt in his hand, the point in its human sheath. At that instant Peyton felt a keen smart in his left leg. It came from a second sabre blow aimed by the Hessian officer, who might have followed it with a third, but that he was now attacked elsewhere. Peyton had no sooner clapped his hand to his wounded leg than he was stunned by a blow from the rifle-butt of the yager who had previously struck the sword. Harry fell forward on the horse's neck, which he grasped madly with both arms, still holding the broken sword in his right hand; and lapsed from a full sense of the tumult, the plunging and shrieking horses, the yelling and cursing men, the whirr and clash of swords, and the thuds of rifle-blows, into blind, red, aching, smarting half-consciousness.

When he was again aware of things, he was still clasping the horse's neck, and was being borne alone he knew not whither. His head ached, and his left leg was at every movement a seat of the sharpest pain. He was dizzy, faint, bleeding, — and too weak to raise himself from his position. He could not hear any noise of fighting, but that might have been drowned by the singing in his ears. He tried to sit up and look around, but the effort so increased his pain and so drew on his nigh-fled strength, that he fell forward on the horse's neck, exhausted and half-insensible. The horse, which had merely turned and run from the conflict at the moment of Peyton's loss of sense, galloped on.

Clouds had darkened the moon in time to prevent their captain's unintentional defection from being seen by his troops. They had, therefore, fought on against such antagonists as, in the darkness, they could keep located. The moon reappeared, and showed many of the Hessians making for the wooded hill near by, and some fleeing to the force that had re-formed further on the road. Some of the Americans charged this force, which thereupon fired a volley and fled, having the more time therefor inasmuch as the charging dragoons did not this time possess their former speed and impetus. The dragoons, in disorder and without a leader, came to a halt. Becoming aware of Peyton's absence, they sought in vain the scene of recent conflict. It was soon inferred that he had been wounded, and, therefore of no further use in the combat, had retreated to a safe resting-place. It was decided useless to follow the enemy further towards the near British posts, whence the Hessians might be reinforced, — as they would have been, had they held the ground longer. So, having had much the better of the fight, the surviving dragoons galloped back towards the post-road, expecting to come upon their captain, wounded, by the wayside, at any moment. He might, indeed, to make sure of safe refuge, ride as far towards the American lines as the wound he must have received would allow him to do.

Such were the doings, on the windy night, beyond Locust Hill, while Elizabeth Philipse and her aunt sat drinking tea by candle-light before a sputtering wood fire. Elizabeth having set the example, the others in the house went about their business, despite the firing so plainly heard. Black Sam had, after Elizabeth's arrival, returned from the orchard, whither he had gone late in the day, lest he might attract the attention of some dodging whale-boat or skulking Whig to the few remaining apples. He had been let in at a rear door by Williams, who had repressed him during the visit of the American dragoons, — for Sam was a sturdy, bold fellow, of different kidney from the dapper, citified Cuff. At

Williams's order he had made a roaring fire in the east parlor, to the great comfort of old Mr. Valentine, and was now putting the dining-room into a similar state of warmth and light. Williams was setting out provisions for Molly presently to cook; and the maid herself was, with Cuff's assistance, replenishing the hall chandelier with fresh candles.

The sound of firing had put Elizabeth's black boy into a tremulous and white-eyed state. When Molly, who stood on the settle while he handed the candles up to her, assured him that the firing was t'other side of Locust Hill, that the bullets would not penetrate the mahogany door, and that anyhow only one bullet in a hundred ever hit any one, Cuff affrightedly observed 'twas just that one bullet he was afraid of; and when, at the third discharge, Molly dropped a candle on his woolly head, he fell prostrate, howling that he was shot. Molly convinced him after awhile that he was alive, but he averred he had actually had a glimpse of the harps and the golden streets, though the prospect of soon possessing them had rather appalled him, as indeed it does many good people who are so sure of heaven and so fond of it. He had been reassured but a short time, when he had new cause for terror. Again a horse was heard galloping up to the house. It stopped before the door and gave a loud whinny.

Molly exchanged with Cuff a look of mingled won-

"LEANED FORWARD ON THE HORSE'S NECK."

der, delight, and doubt; then ran and opened the front door.

"Yes!" she cried. "It is! It's Miss Elizabeth's horse! It's Cato!"

Cuff ran to the threshold in great joy, but suddenly stopped short.

"Dey's a soldier on hees back," he whispered.

So Molly had noticed, — but a soldier who made no demonstration, a soldier who leaned forward on the horse's neck and clutched its mane, holding at the same time in one hand a broken sword, and who tried to sit up, but only emitted a groan of pain.

"He's wounded, that's it," said Molly. "Go and help the poor soldier in, Cuff. Don't you see he's injured? He can't hurt you."

Molly enforced her commands with such physical persuasions that Cuff, ere he well knew what he was about, was helping Peyton from the horse. The captain, revived by a supreme effort, leaned on the boy's shoulder and came limping and lurching across the porch into the hall. Molly then went to his assistance, and with this additional aid he reached the settle, on which he dropped, weak, pale, and panting. He took a sitting posture, gasped his thanks to Molly, and, noticing the blood from his leg wound, called damnation on the Hessian officer's sword. Presently he asked for a drink of water.

At Molly's bidding the negro boy hastened for

water, and also to inform his mistress of the arrival. Elizabeth, hearing the news, rose with an exclamation ; but, taking thought, sat down again, and, with a pretence of composure, finished her cup of tea. Cuff returned with a glass of water to the hall, where Molly was listening to Peyton's objurgations on his condition. The captain took the glass eagerly, and was about to drink, when a footstep was heard on the stairs. He turned his head and saw Elizabeth.

" Here's my respects, madam," quoth he, and drank off the water.

Elizabeth came down-stairs and took a position where she could look Peyton well over. He watched her with some wonderment. When she was quite ready she spoke :

" So, it is, indeed, the man who stole my horse."

" Pardon. I think your horse has stolen *me !* It made me an intruder here quite against my will, I assure you."

" You will doubtless not honor us by remaining ?" There was more seriousness of curiosity in this question than Elizabeth betrayed or Peyton perceived.

" What can I do ? I can neither ride nor walk."

" But your men will probably come for you ?"

" I don't think any saw the horse bear me from the fight. The field was in smoke and darkness. My troops must have pursued the enemy. They'll think me killed or made prisoner. If they return this way, however, I can have them stop and take me along."

"Then you expect that, in repayment of your treatment of me awhile ago —" Elizabeth paused.

"Madam, you should allow for the exigencies of war! Yet, if you wish to turn me out —"

Elizabeth interrupted him :

"So it is true that, if you fell into the hands of the British, they would hang you ?"

"Doubtless! But you shouldn't blame *me* for what *they'd* do. And how did you know?"

"Help this gentleman into the east parlor," said Elizabeth, abruptly, to Cuff.

"Ah!" cried Peyton, his face lighting up with quick gratitude. "Madam, you then make me your guest?" He thrust forward his head, forgetful of his condition.

"My guest ?" rang out Elizabeth's voice in answer. "You insolent rebel, I intend to hand you over to the British!"

There was a brief silence. Each gazed at the other.

"You will not — do that ?" said Peyton, in a voice little above a whisper.

"Wait and see!" And she stood regarding him with elation.

He stared at her in blank consternation.

Again, the sound of the trample of many horses.

"Ah!" cried Peyton, joyfully. "My men returning!"

He rose to go to the door, but his wounded leg gave way, and he staggered to the staircase, and leaned against the balustrade.

Elizabeth's look of gratification faded. She ran to the door, fastened it with bolt and key, and stood with her back against it.

The sound, first distant as if in the Mile Square road, was now manifestly in the highway. Would it come southward, towards the house, or go northward, decreasing?

"They are my men!" cried Peyton to Cuff. "Call them! They'll pass without knowing I am here. Call them, I say! Quick! They'll be out of hearing."

"Silence!" said Elizabeth to Cuff, in a low tone, and stood listening.

Peyton made another attempt to move, but realized his inability. 'Twas all he could do to support himself against the balustrade.

"My God, they've gone by!" he cried. "They'll return to our lines, leaving me behind." And he shouted, "Carrington!"

The voice rang for a moment in the remoteness of the hall above. Then complete silence within. All in the hall remained motionless, listening. The sound of the horses came fainter and fainter.

"Carrington! Help! I'm in the manor-house, — a prisoner!"

A look of despair came over his face. On Elizabeth's the suspense gave way to a smile of triumph.

The sound of the horses died away.

CHAPTER VI.

THE ONE CHANCE.

PEYTON staggered back to the settle and sank down on it, exhausted. Elizabeth, hearing black Sam moving about in the dining-room, which was directly north of the hall, bade Molly summon him. When he appeared, she ordered him and Cuff to carry the settle, with the wounded man on it, into the east parlor, and to place the man on the sofa there. She then told Molly to hasten the supper, and to send Williams to her up-stairs, and thereupon rejoined her excited aunt above. When Williams attended her, she gave him commands regarding the prisoner.

Peyton was thus carried through the deep doorway in the south side of the hall into the east parlor, which was now exceedingly habitable with fire roaring and candles lighted. In the east and south sides of this richly ornamented room were deeply embrasured windows, with low seats. In the west side was a mahogany door opening from the old or south hall. In the north side, which was adorned with wooden pillars and other carved woodwork, was the door through which Peyton had been carried; west of that, the decorated chimney-breast with its English mantel and fireplace, and further west a pair of doors opening from a closet, whence a winding staircase descended cellarward. The ceiling was rich with fanciful arabesque woodwork. Set in the chimney-breast, over the mantel, was an oblong mirror. The wainscoting, pillars, and other woodwork were of a creamy white. But Peyton had no eye for details at the moment. He noticed only that his entrance disturbed the slumbers of the old gentleman — Matthias Valentine — who had been sleeping in a great armchair by the fire, and who now blinked in wonderment.

The negroes put down the settle and lifted Peyton to a sofa that stood against the western side of the room, between a spinet and the northern wall. At Peyton's pantomimic request they then moved the sofa to a place near the fire, and then, taking the settle along, marched out of the room, back to the hall, closing the door as they went.

Peyton, too pain-racked and exhausted to speak, lay back on the sofa, with closed eyes. Old Valentine stared at him a few moments; then, curious both as to this unexpected advent and as to the proximity of supper, rose and hobbled from the parlor and across the hall to the dining-room. For some time Peyton was left alone. He opened his eyes, studied the flying figures on the ceiling, the portraits on the walls, the carpet, — Philipse Manor-house, like the best English houses of the time, had carpet on its floors, — the carving of the mantel, the clock and candelabrum thereupon, the crossed rapiers thereabove, the curves of the imported furniture. His twinges and aches were so many and so diverse that he made no attempt to locate them separately. He could feel that the left leg of his breeches was soaked with blood.

Finally the door opened, and in came Williams and Cuff, the former with shears and bands of linen, the latter with a basin of water. Williams, whom Peyton had not before seen, scrutinized him critically, and forthwith proceeded to expose, examine, wash, and bind up the wounded leg, while Cuff stood by and played the rôle of surgeon's assistant. Peyton speedily perceived on the steward's part a reliable acquaintance with the art of dressing cuts, and therefore submitted without a word to his operations. Williams was equally silent, breaking his reticence only now and then to utter some monosyllabic command to Cuff.

When the wound was dressed, Williams put the patient's disturbed attire to rights, and adjusted his hair. Peyton, with a feeling of some relief, made to stretch the wounded leg, but a sharp twinge cut the movement short.

"You should make a good surgeon," Peyton said at last, "you tie so damnably tight a bandage."

"I've bound up many a wound, sir," said Williams; "and some far worse than yours. 'Tis not a dangerous cut, yours, though 'twill be irritating while it lasts. You won't walk for a day or two."

"It's remarkable your mistress has so much trouble taken with me, when she intends to deliver me to the British."

Peyton had inferred the steward's place in the house, from his appearance and manner.

"Why, sir," said Williams, "we couldn't have you bleeding over the floor and furniture. Besides, I suppose she wants to hand you over in good condition."

"I see! No bedraggled remnant of a man, but a complete, clean, and comfortable candidate for Cunningham's gallows!" Peyton here forgot his wound and attempted to sit upright, but quickly fell back with a grimace and a groan.

"Better lie still, sir," counselled Williams, sagely. "If you need any one, you are to call Cuff. He will be in waiting in that hall, sir." And the steward pointed towards the east hall. "There will be no use trying to get away. I doubt if you could walk half across the room without fainting. And if you could get out of the house, you'd find black Sam on guard, with his duck-gun, — and Sam doesn't miss once in a hundred times with that duck-gun. Bring those things, Cuff." Williams indicated Peyton's hat, remnant of sword, and scabbard, which had been placed on the armchair by the fireside.

"Leave my sword!" commanded Peyton.

"Can't, sir!" said Williams, affably. "Miss Elizabeth's orders were to take it away."

Williams thereupon went from the room, crossed the east hall, and entered the dining-room, to report to Elizabeth, who now sat at supper with Miss Sally and Mr. Valentine.

Cuff, with basin of water in one hand, took up the hat, sword, and scabbard, with the other.

"Miss Elizabeth!" mused Peyton. "Queen Elizabeth, I should say, in this house. Gad, to be a girl's prisoner, tied down to a sofa by so small a cut!" Hereupon he addressed Cuff, who was about to depart : "Where is your mistress?"

"In the dining-room, eating supper."

"And Mr. Colden, whom I saw in that hall about an hour ago, when I bought the horse?"

"Major Colden rode back to New York."

"*Major* Colden! Major of what?"

"New Juzzey Vollingteers, sir."

"What? Then he is in the King's service, after all? And when I was here with my troops he said he was neutral. I'll never take a Tory's word again."

"Am you like to hab de chance, sir?" queried Cuff, with a grin.

"What! You taunt me with my situation?" And Harry's head shot up from the sofa as he made to rise and chastise the boy; but he could not stand on his leg, and so remained sitting, propped on his right arm, panting and glaring at the negro.

Cuff, whose whiteness of teeth had shown in his moment of mirth, now displayed much whiteness of eye in his alarm at Peyton's movement, and glided to the door. As he went out to the hall, he passed Molly, who was coming into the parlor with a bowl of broth.

"Hah!" ejaculated Peyton as she came towards him. "They would feed the animal for the slaughter, eh?"

Molly curtseyed.

"Please, sir, it wa'n't they sent this. I brought it of my own accord, sir, though with Miss Elizabeth's permission."

"Oh! so Miss Elizabeth *did* give her permission, then?"

"Yes, sir. At least, she said it didn't matter, if I wished to."

"And you did wish to? Well, you're a good girl, and I thank you."

Whereupon Peyton took the bowl and sipped of the broth with relish.

"Thank you, sir," said Molly, who then moved a small light chair from its place by the wall to a spot beside the sofa and within Peyton's reach. "You can set the bowl on this," she added. "I must go back to the kitchen." And, after another curtsey, she was gone.

The broth revived Peyton, and with all his pain and fatigue he had some sense of comfort. The handsome, well warmed, well lighted parlor, so richly furnished, so well protected from the wind and weather by the solid shutters outside its four small-paned windows, was certainly a snug corner of the world. So far seemed all this from stress and war, that Peyton lost his strong realization of the fate that Elizabeth's threat promised him. Appreciation of his surroundings drove away other thoughts and feelings. That he should be taken and hanged was an idea so remote from his present situation, it seemed rather like a dream than an imminent reality. There surely would be a way of his getting hence in safety. And he imbibed mouthful after mouthful of the warm broth.

Presently old Mr. Valentine reappeared, from the east hall, looking none the less comfortable for the supper he had eaten. A long pipe was in his hand, and, that he might absorb smoke and liquor at the same time, he had brought with him from the table, where the two ladies remained, a vast mug of hot rum punch of Williams's brewing. He now set the mug on the mantel, lighted his pipe with a brand from the fire, repossessed himself of the mug, and sat down in the armchair, with a sigh of huge satisfaction. It mattered not that this was the parlor of Philipse Manor-house, — for Mr. Valentine, in his innocent way, indulged himself freely in the privileges and presumptions of old age.

Peyton, after staring for some time with curiosity at the smoky old gentleman, who rapidly grew smokier, at last raised the bowl of broth for a last gulp, saying, cheerily:

"To your very good health, sir!"

"Thank you, sir!" said the old man, complacently, not making any movement to reciprocate.

"What! won't you drink to mine?"

"'Twould be a waste of words to drink the health of a man that's going to be hanged," replied Valentine, who at supper had heard the ladies discuss Peyton's intended fate. He thereupon sent a cloud of smoke ceiling-ward for the flying cherubs to rest on.

"The devil! You *are* economical!"

"Of words, maybe, not of liquor." The octogenarian quaffed deeply from the mug. "They say hanging is an easy death," he went on, being in loquacious mood. "I never saw but one man hanged. He didn't seem to enjoy it." Mr. Valentine puffed slowly, inwardly dwelling on the recollection.

"Oh, didn't he?" said Peyton.

"No, he took it most unpleasant like."

"Did you come in here to cheer me up in my last hours?" queried Harry, putting the empty bowl on the chair by the sofa.

"No," replied the other, ingenuously. "I came in for a smoke while the ladies stayed at the table." He then went back to a subject that seemed to have attractions for him. "I don't know how hanging will go with you. Cunningham will do the work.[5] They say he makes it as disagreeable as may be. I'd come and see you hanged, but it won't be possible."

"Then I suppose I shall have to excuse you," said Peyton, with resignation.

"Yes." The old man had finished his punch and set down his mug, and he now yawned with a completeness that revealed vastly more of red toothless mouth than one might have calculated his face could contain. "Some take it easier than others," he went on. "It's harder with young men like you." Again he opened his jaws in a gape as whole-souled as that of a house-dog before a kitchen fire. "It must be disagreeable to have a rope tightened around your neck. I don't know." He thrust his pipe-stem absently between his lips, closed his eyes, mumbled absently, "I don't know," and in a few moments was asleep, his pipe hanging from his mouth, his hands folded in his lap.

"A cheerful companion for a man in my situation," thought Peyton. His mind had been brought back to the future. When would this resolute and vengeful Miss Elizabeth fulfil her threat? How would she proceed about it? Had she already taken measures towards his conveyance to the British lines? Should she delay until he should be able to walk, there would be two words about the matter. Meanwhile, he must wait for developments. It was useless to rack his brain with conjectures. His sense of present comfort gradually resumed sway, and he placed his head again on the sofa pillow and closed his eyes.

He was conscious for a time of nothing but his deadened pain, his inward comfort, the breathing of old Mr. Valentine, the intermittent raging of the wind without, and the steady ticking of the clock on the mantel, — which delicately framed timepiece had been started within the hour by Sam, who knew Miss Elizabeth's will for having all things in running order. Peyton's drowsiness wrapped him closer and closer. Presently he was remotely aware of the opening of the door, the tread of light feet on the floor, the swish of skirts. But he had now reached that lethargic point which involves total indifference to outer things, and he did not even open his eyes.

"Asleep," said Elizabeth, for it was she who had entered with her aunt.

Harry recognized the voice, and knew that he was the subject of her remark; but his feeling towards his contemptuous captor was not such as to make him take the trouble of setting her right. Therefore, he kept his eyes closed, having a kind of satisfaction in her being mistaken.

"How handsome!" whispered Miss Sally, who beamed more bigly and benignly after supper than before.

"Which one, aunty?" said Elizabeth, looking from Peyton to old Valentine.

Her aunt deigned to this levity only a look of hopeless reproof.

Elizabeth sat down on the music-seat before the spinet, and became serious, — or, more accurately, businesslike.

"On second thought," said she, "it won't do to keep him here waiting for one of our patrols to pass this way. In the meantime some of the rebels might come into the neighborhood and stop here. He must be delivered to the British this very night!"

Peyton gave no outward sign of the momentary heart stoppage he felt within.

"Why," said the aunt, speaking low, and in some alarm, "'twould require Williams and both the blacks to take him, and we should be left alone in the house."

"I sha'n't send him to the troops," said Elizabeth,

in her usual tone, not caring whether or not the prisoner should be disturbed, — for in his powerlessness he could not oppose her plans if he did know them, and in her disdain she had no consideration for his feelings. "The troops shall come for him. Black Sam shall go to the watch-house at King's Bridge with word that there's an important rebel prisoner held here, to be had for the taking."

"Will the troops at King's Bridge heed the story of a black man?" Aunt Sally seemed desirous of interposing objections to immediate action.

"Their officer will heed a written message from me," said the niece. "Most of the officers know me, and those at King's Bridge are aware I came here to-day."

Thereupon she called in Cuff, and sent him off for Williams, with orders that the steward should bring her pen, ink, paper, and wax.

"Oh, Elizabeth!" cried Miss Sally, looking at the floor. "Here's some of the poor fellow's blood on the carpet."

"Never mind. The blood of an enemy is a sight easily tolerated," said the girl, probably unaware how nearly she had duplicated a famous utterance of a certain King of France, whose remark had borne reference to another sense than that of sight.[6]

Williams soon came in with the writing materials, and placed them, at Elizabeth's direction, on a table that stood between the two eastern windows, and on which was a lighted candelabrum. Elizabeth sat down at the table, her back towards the fireplace and ⁕Peyton.

"I wish you to send black Sam to me," said she to the steward, "and to take his place on guard with the gun till he returns from an errand."

Williams departed, and Elizabeth began to make the quill fly over the paper, her aunt looking on from beside the table. Peyton opened his eyes and looked at them.

"It does seem a pity," said Miss Sally at last. "Such a pretty gentleman, — such a gallant soldier!"

"Gentleman?" echoed Elizabeth, writing on. "The fellow is not a gentleman! Nor a gallant soldier!"

Peyton rose to a sitting posture as if stung by a hornet, but was instantly reminded of his wound. But neither Elizabeth nor her aunt saw or heard his movement. The girl, unaware that he was awake, continued:

"Does a gentleman or a gallant soldier desert the army of his king to join that of his king's enemies?"

Quick came the answer, — not from aunt Sally, but from Peyton on the sofa.

"A gallant soldier has the right to choose his side, and a gentleman need not fight against his country!"

Elizabeth did not suffer herself to appear startled at this sudden breaking in. Having finished her note, she quietly folded it, and addressed it, while she said :

"A gallant soldier, having once chosen his side, will be loyal to it ; and a gentleman never bore the odious title of deserter."

"A gentleman can afford to wear any title that is redeemed by a glorious cause and an extraordinary danger. When I took service with the King's army in England, I never dreamt that army would be sent against the King's own colonies; and not till I arrived in Boston did I know the true character of this revolt. We thought we were coming over merely to quell a lawless Boston rabble. I gave in my resignation — "

"But did not wait for it to be accepted," interrupted Elizabeth, quietly, as she applied to the folded paper the wax softened by the flame of a candle.

"I *was* a little hasty," said Harry.

"The rebel army was the proper place for such fellows," said Elizabeth. "No true British officer would be guilty of such a deed!"

"Probably not! It required exceptional courage!"

Peyton knew, as well as any, that the British were brave enough ; but he was in mood for sharp retort.

"That is not the reason," said Elizabeth, coldly,

refusing to show wrath. "Your enemies hold such acts as yours in detestation."

"I am not serving in this war for the approbation of my enemies."

At this moment black Sam came in. Elizabeth handed him the letter, and said :

"You are to take my horse Cato, and ride with this message to the British barrier at King's Bridge. It is for the officer in command there. When the sentries challenge you, show this, and say it is of the greatest consequence and must be delivered at once."

"Yes, Miss Elizabeth."

"The commander," she went on, "will probably send here a body of troops at once, to convey this prisoner within the lines. You are to return with them. If no time is lost, and they send mounted troops, you should be back in an hour."

Peyton could hardly repress a start.

"An hour at most, miss, if nothing stops," said the negro.

"If any officer of my acquaintance is in command," said Elizabeth, "there will be no delay. Cuff shall let the troops in, through that hall, as soon as they arrive."

Whereupon the black man, a stalwart and courageous specimen of his race, went rapidly from the room.

"One hour!" murmured Peyton, looking at the clock.

Molly, the maid, now reappeared, carrying carefully in one hand a cup, from which a thin steam ascended.

"What is't now, Molly?" inquired Elizabeth, rising from her chair.

Molly blushed and was much confused. "Tea, ma'am, if you please! I thought, maybe, you'd allow the gentleman —"

"Very well," said Elizabeth. "Be the good Samaritan if you like, child. His tea-drinking days will soon be over. Come, aunt Sally, we shall be in better company elsewhere." And she returned to the dining-room, not deigning her prisoner another look.

Miss Sally followed, but her feelings required confiding in some one, and before she went she whispered to the embarrassed maid, "Oh, Molly, to think so sweet a young gentleman should be completely wasted!"

Molly heaved a sigh, and then approached the young gentleman himself, with whom she was now alone, saving the presence of the slumbering Valentine.

"So your name is Molly? And you've brought me tea this time?"

"Yes, sir, — if you please, sir." She took up the bowl from the chair and placed the cup in its stead. "I put sugar in this, sir, but if you'd rather —"

"I'd rather have it just as you've made it, Molly,"

he said, in a singularly gentle, unsteady tone. He raised the cup, and sipped. "Delicious, Molly! — Hah! Your mistress thinks my tea-drinking days will soon be over."

"I'm very sorry, sir."

"So am I." He held the cup in his left hand, supporting his upright body with his right arm, and looked rather at vacancy than at the maid. "Never to drink tea again," he said, "or wine or spirits, for that matter! To close your eyes on this fine world! Never again to ride after the hounds, or sing, or laugh, or chuck a pretty girl under the chin!"

And here, having set down the cup, he chucked Molly herself under the chin, pretending a gaiety he did not feel.

"Never again," he went on, "to lead a charge against the enemies of our liberty ; not to live to see this fight out, the King's regiments driven from the land, the States take their place among the free nations of the world! *By God, Molly, I don't want to die yet !*"

It was not the fear of death, it was the love of life, and what life might have in reserve, that moved him ; and it now asserted itself in him with a force tenfold greater than ever before. Death, — or, rather, the ceasing of life, — as he viewed it now, when he was like to meet it without company, with prescribed preliminaries, in an ignominious mode, was a far other thing than as viewed in the exaltation of battle, when a man chances it hot-headed, uplifted, thrilled, in gallant comradeship, to his own fate rendered careless by a sense of his nothingness in comparison with the whole vast drama. Moreover, in going blithely to possible death in open fight, one accomplishes something for his cause; not so, going unwillingly to certain death on an enemy's gallows. It was, too, an exasperating thought that he should die to gratify the vengeful whim of an insolent Tory girl.

"Will it really come to that?" asked Molly, in a frightened tone.

"As surely as I fall into British hands!"

Peyton remembered the case of General Charles Lee, whose resignation of half-pay had not been acknowledged; who was, when captured by the British, long in danger of hanging, and who was finally rated as an ordinary war prisoner only for Washington's threat to retaliate on five Hessian field officers. If a major-general, whose desertion, even if admitted, was from half-pay only, would have been hanged without ceremony but for General Howe's fear of a "law scrape," and had been saved from shipment to England for trial, only by the King's fear that Washington's retaliation would disaffect the Hessian allies, for what could a mere captain look, who had come over from the enemy in action, and whose punishment would entail no official retaliation?

"And your mistress expects a troop of British soldiers here in an hour to take me! Damn it, if I could only walk!" And he looked rapidly around the room, in a kind of distraction, as if seeking some means of escape. Realizing the futility of this, he sighed dismally, and drank the remainder of the tea.

"You couldn't get away from the house, sir," said Molly. "Williams is watching outside."

"I'd take a chance if I could only run!" Peyton muttered. He had no fear that Molly would betray him. "If there were some hiding-place I might crawl to! But the troops would search every cranny about the house." He turned to Molly suddenly, seeing, in his desperate state and his lack of time, but one hope. "I wonder, could Williams be bribed to spirit me away?"

Molly's manner underwent a slight chill.

"Oh, no," said she. "He'd die before he'd disobey Miss Elizabeth. We all would, sir. I'm very sorry, indeed, sir." Whereupon, taking up the empty bowl and teacup, she hastened from the room.

Peyton sat listening to the clock-ticks. He moved his right leg so that the foot rested on the floor, then tried to move the left one after it, using his hand to guide it. With great pains and greater pain, he finally got the left foot beside the right. He then undertook to stand, but the effort cost him such physical agony as could not be borne for any length of time. He fell back with a groan to the sofa, convinced that the wounded leg was not only, for the time, useless itself, but also an impediment to whatever service the other leg might have rendered alone. But he remained sitting up, his right foot on the floor.

Suddenly there was a raucous sound from old Mr. Valentine. He had at last begun to snore. But this infliction brought its own remedy, for when his jaws opened wider his tobacco pipe fell from his mouth and struck his folded hands. He awoke with a start, and blinked wonderingly at Peyton, whose face, turned towards the old man, still wore the look of disapproval evoked by the momentary snoring.

"Still here, eh?" piped Mr. Valentine. "I dreamt you were being hanged to the fireplace, like a pig to be smoked. I was quite upset over it! Such a fine young gentleman, and one of Harry Lee's officers, too!"

And the old man shook his head deploringly.

"Then why don't you help me out of this?" demanded Peyton, whose impulse was for grasping at straws, for he thought of black Sam urging Cato through the wind towards King's Bridge at a gallop.

"It ain't possible," said Valentine, phlegmatically.

"If it were, would you?" asked Harry, a spark of

hope igniting from the appearance that the old man
was, at least, not antagonistic to him.

"Why, yes," began the octogenarian, placidly.
Harry's heart bounded.

"If," the old man went on, "I could without
lending aid to the King's enemies. But you see I
couldn't. I won't lend aid to neither side's enemies.
I don't want to die afore my time." And he gazed
complacently at the fire.

Peyton knew the hopeless immovability of selfish
old age.

"God!" he muttered, in despair. "Is there no
one I can turn to?"

"There's none within hearing would dare go
against the orders of Miss Elizabeth," said Mr.
Valentine.

"Miss Elizabeth evidently rules with a firm hand,"
said Peyton, bitterly. "Her word —" He stopped
suddenly, as if struck by a new thought. "If I
could but move *her!* If I could make her change
her mind!"

"You couldn't. No one ever could, and as for a
rebel soldier —"

"She has a heart of iron, that girl!" broke in
Peyton. "The cruelty of a savage!"

Mr. Valentine took on a sincerely deprecating
look. "Oh, you mustn't abuse Miss Elizabeth,"
said he. "It ain't cruelty, it's only proper pride.

And she isn't hard.   She has the kindest heart, —
to those she's fond of."

"To those she's fond of," repeated Harry, mechanically.

"Yes," said the old man ; "her people, her horses,
her dogs and cats, and even her servants and slaves."

"Tender creature, who has a heart for a dog and
not for a man !"

The old man's loyalty to three generations of
Philipses made him a stubborn defender, and he
answered :

"She'd have no less a heart for a man if she
loved him."

"If she loved him !" echoed Peyton, and began to
think.

"Ay, and a thousand times more heart, loving
him as a woman loves a man." Mr. Valentine
spoke knowingly, as one acquainted by enviable
experience with the measure of such love.

"As a woman loves a man !" repeated Peyton.
Suddenly he turned to Valentine.   "Tell me, does
she love any man so, now ?"   Peyton did not know
the relation in which Elizabeth and Major Colden
stood to each other.

"I can't say she *loves* one," replied Valentine,
judicially, "though — "

But Peyton had heard enough.

"By heaven, I'll try it !" he cried.   "Such

miracles have happened ! And I have almost an hour ! "

Old Valentine blinked at him, with stupid lack of perception. "What is it, sir?"

"I shall try it!" was Peyton's unenlightening answer. "There's one chance. And you can help me!"

"The devil I can!" replied Valentine, rising from his chair in some annoyance. "I won't lend aid, I tell you!"

"It won't be 'lending aid.' All I beg is that you ask Miss Elizabeth to see me alone at once, — and that you'll forget all I've said to you. Don't stand staring! For Christ's sake, go and ask her to come in! Don't you know? Only an hour, — less than that, now!"

"But she mayn't come here for the asking," objected the old man, somewhat dazed by Peyton's petulance.

"She *must* come here!" cried Harry. "Induce her, beg her, entice her! Tell her I have a last request to make of my jailer, — no, excite her curiosity; tell her I have a confession to make, a plot to disclose, — anything! In heaven's name, go and send her here!"

It was easier to comply with so light a request than to remain recipient of such torrent-like importunity. "I'll try, sir," said the peace-loving old man, "but I have no hope," and he hobbled from the room. He left the door open as he went, and Harry, tortured by impatience, heard him shuffling over the hall floor to the dining-room.

Peyton's mind was in a whirl. He glanced at the clock. These were his thoughts :

"Fifty minutes! To make a woman love me! A proud woman, vain and wilful, who hates our cause, who detests me! To make her love me! How shall I begin? Keep your wits now, Harry, my son, — 'tis for your life! How to begin? Why doesn't she come? Damn the clock, how loud it ticks! I feel each tick. No, 'tis my heart I feel. My God, *will* she not come? And the time is going —"

"Well, sir, what is it?"

He looked from the clock to the doorway, where stood Elizabeth.

CHAPTER VII

THE FLIGHT OF THE MINUTES.

THE silence of her entrance was from her having, a few minutes earlier, exchanged her riding-boots for satin slippers.

"I — I thank you for coming, madam," said Peyton, feeling the necessity of a prompt reply to her imperious look of inquiry, yet without a practicable idea in his head. "I had — that is — a request to make."

He was trembling violently, not from fear, but from that kind of agitation which often precedes the undertaking of a critical task, as when a suppliant awaits an important interview, or an actor assumes for the first time a new part.

"Mr. Valentine said a confession," said Elizabeth, holding him in a coldly resentful gaze.

"Why, yes, a confession," said he, hopelessly.

"A plot to disclose," she added, with sharp impatience. "What is it?"

"You shall hear," he began, in gloomy desperation, without the faintest knowledge of how he should finish. "I — ah — it is this — " His wandering glance fell on the table and the writing materials she had left there. "I wish to write a letter — a last letter — to a friend." The vague general outline of a project arose in his mind.

Elizabeth was inclined to be as laconic as implacable. "Write it," said she. "There are pen and ink."

"But I can't write in this position," said Peyton, quickly, lest she might leave the room. "I fear I can't even hold a pen. Will you not write for me?"

"I? Secretary to a horse-thieving rebel!"

"It is a last request, madam. A last request is sacred, — even an enemy's."

"I will send in some one to write for you." And she turned to go.

"But this letter will contain secrets."

"Secrets?" The very word is a charm to a woman. Elizabeth's curiosity was touched but slightly, yet sufficiently to stay her steps for the moment.

"Ay," said Peyton, lowering his tone and speaking quickly, "secrets not for every ear. Secrets of the heart, madam, — secrets so delicate that, to convey them truly, I need the aid of more than common tact and understanding."

He watched her eagerly, and tried to repress the signs of his anxiety.

Elizabeth considered for a moment, then went to the table and sat down by it.

"But," said she, regarding him with angry suspicion, "the confession, — the plot?"

"Why, madam," said he, his heart hammering forcefully, "do you think I may communicate them to you directly? The letter shall relate them, too, and if the person who holds the pen for me pays heed to the letter's contents, is it my fault?"

"I understand," said the woman, entrapped, and she dipped the quill into the ink.

"The letter," began Peyton, slowly, hesitating for ideas, and glancing at the clock, yet not retaining a sense of where the hands were, "is to Mr. Bryan Fairfax —"

"What?" she interrupted. "Kinsman to Lord Fairfax, of Virginia?"

"There's but one Mr. Bryan Fairfax," said Peyton, acquiring confidence from his preliminary expedient to overcome prejudice, "and, though he's on the side of King George in feeling, yet he's my friend, — a circumstance that should convince even you I'm not scum o' the earth, rebel though you call me. He's the friend of Washington, too."

"Poh! Who is your Washington? My aunt Mary rejected him, and married his rival in this very room!"

"And a good thing Washington didn't marry

her!" said Peyton, gallantly. "She'd have tried to turn him Tory, and the ladies of this family are not to be resisted."

"Go on with your letter," said Elizabeth, chillingly.

"'Mr. Bryan Fairfax,'" dictated Peyton, steadying his voice with an effort, "'Towlston Hall, Fairfax County, Virginia. My dear Fairfax: If ever these reach you, 'twill be from out a captivity destined, probably, to end soon in that which all dread, yet to which all must come; a captivity, nevertheless, sweetened by the divinest presence that ever bore the name of woman —'"

Elizabeth stopped writing, and looked up, with an astonishment so all-possessing that it left no room even for indignation.

Peyton, his eyes astray in the preoccupation of composition, did not notice her look, but, as if moved by enthusiasm, rose on his right leg and stood, his hands placed on the back of the light chair by the sofa, the chair's front being turned from him. He went on, with an affectation of repressed rapture: "''Twere worth even death to be for a short hour the prisoner of so superb —'"

"Sir, what are you saying?" And Elizabeth dropped the pen, and stood up, regarding him with freezing resentment.

"My thoughts, madam," said he, humbly, meeting her gaze.

"How dare you jest with me?" said she.

"Jest? Does a man jest in the face of his own death?"

"'Twas a jest to bid me write such lies!"

"Lies? 'Fore gad, the mirror yonder will not call them lies!" He indicated the oblong glass set in above the mantel. "If there is lying, 'tis my eyes that lie! 'Tis only what they tell me, that my lips report."

Keeping his left foot slightly raised from the floor, he pushed the chair a little towards her, and himself followed it, resting his weight partly on its back, while he hopped with his right foot. But Elizabeth stayed him with a gesture of much imperiousness.

"What has such rubbish to do with your confession and your plot?" she demanded.

"Can you not see?" And he now let some of his real agitation appear, that it might serve as the lover's perturbation which it would be well to display.

"My confession is of the instant yielding of my heart to the charms of a goddess."

In those days lovers, real or pretended, still talked of goddesses, flames, darts, and such.

"Who desired your heart to yield to anything?" was Miss Elizabeth's sharply spoken reply.

"Beauty *commanded* it, madam!" said he, bowing low over his chair-back.

"So, then, there was no plot?" Her eyes flashed with indignation.

"A plot, yes!" He glanced sidewise at the clock, and drew self-reliance from the very situation, which began to intoxicate him. "*My* plot, to attract you hither, by that message, that I might console myself for my fate by the joy of seeing you!"

"The joy of seeing me!" She spoke with incredulity and contempt.

A glad boldness had come over Peyton. He felt himself masterful, as one feels who is drunk with wine; yet, unlike such a one, he had command of mind and body.

"Ay, joy," said he, "joy none the less that you are disdainful! Pride is the attribute of queens, and tenderness is not the only mood in which a woman may conquer. Heaven! You can so discomfit a man with your frowns, *what* might you do with your smile!"

He felt now that he could dissimulate to fool the very devil.

But Elizabeth, though interested as one may be in an oddity, seemed not otherwise impressed. 'Twas something, however, that she remained in the room to answer :

"I do not know what I have done with my frown, nor what I might do with my smile, but, whatever it be, *you* are not like to see!"

"That I know," said Peyton, and added, at a reckless venture, "and am consoled, when I consider that no other man has seen!"

"How do you know that?"

"Your smile is not for any common man, and I'll wager your heart is as whole as your beauty."

She looked at him for a moment of silence, then:

"I cannot imagine why you say all this," quoth she, in real puzzlement.

"'Tis an easing to the tortured heart to reveal itself," he answered, "as one would fain uncover an inner wound, though there be no hope of cure. I can go the calmer to my doom for having at least given outlet in words to the flame kindled in a moment within me. My doom! Yes, and none so unwelcome, either, if by it I escape a lifetime of vain longing!"

"Your talk is incomprehensible, sir. If you are serious, it must be that your head is turned."

"My head is turned, doubtless, but by you!"

He was now assuming the low, quick, nervous utterance that is often associated with intense repressed feeling; and his words were accompanied by his best possible counterfeit of the burning, piercing, distraught gaze of passion. Though he acted a part, it was not with the cold-blooded art of a mimic who simulates by rule; it was with the animation due to imagining himself actually swayed by the feeling he would feign. While he *knew* his emotion to be fictitious, he *felt* it as if it were real, and his consequent actions were the same as if real it were.

"I'm sure the act was not intentional with me," said Elizabeth. "I'd best leave you, lest you grow worse." And she moved towards the door.

Peyton had rapid work of it, pushing the chair before him and hopping after it, so as to intercept her. In the excitement of the moment, he lost his mastery of himself.

"But you must not go! Hear me, I beg! Good God, only a half hour left!"

"A half hour?" repeated Elizabeth, inquiringly.

"I mean," said Peyton, recovering his wits, "a half hour till the troops may be here for me, — only a half hour until I must leave your house forever! Do not let me be deprived of the sight of you for those last minutes! 'Tis so short a time, yet 'tis all my life!"

"The man is mad, I think!" She spoke as if to herself.

"Mad!" he echoed. "Yes, some do call it a madness — the love that's born of a glance, and lasts till death!"

"Love!" said she. "'Tis impossible you should come to love me, in so short a time."

"'Tis born of a glance, I tell you!" he cried. "What is it, if not love, that makes me forget my coming death, see only you, hear only you, think of only you? Why do I not spend this time, this last hour, in pleading for my life, in begging you to hide me and send the troops away without me when they come? They would take your word, and you are a woman, and women are moved by pleading. Why, then, do I not, in the brief time I have left, beg for my life? Because my passion blinds me to all else, because I would use every moment in pouring out my heart to you, because my feelings must have outlet in words, because it is more than life or death to me that you should know I love you! — God, how fast that clock goes!"

She had stood in wonderment, under the spell of his vehemence. Now, as he leaned towards her, over the chair-back, his breath coming rapidly, his eyes luminous, she seemed for a moment abashed, softened, subdued. But she put to flight his momentary hope by starting again for the doorway, with a low-spoken, "I must go!"

But he thrust his chair in her way.

"Nay, don't go!" he said. "You may hear my avowal with propriety. My people are as good as any in Virginia."

She stood regarding him with a look of scrutiny.

"You are a rebel against your king," she said, but not harshly.

"Is not the King soon to have his revenge?

And is that a reason why you should leave me now ? "

" You deserted your first colors."

"'Twas in extraordinary circumstances, and in the right cause.   And is that a reason why you — "

" You took my horse."

" But paid you for it, and you have your horse again.   Abuse me, madam, but do not go from me. Call me rebel, deserter, robber, what you will, but remain with me.   Denunciation from your lips 'is sweeter than praise from others.   Chastise me, strike me, trample on me, — I shall worship you none the less ! "

He inclined his body further forward over the chair-back, and thus was very near her.   She put out her hand to repel him.   He moved back with humility, but took her hand and kissed it, with an appearance of passion qualified by reverence.

" How dare you touch my hand ? "   And she quickly drew it from him.

" A poor wretch who loves, and is soon to die, dares much ! "

" You seem resigned to dying," she remarked.

" Have I not said 'tis better than living with a hopeless passion ? "

" And yet death," she said, "*that* kind of a death is not pleasant."

" I'm not afraid of it," said he, wondering how the

minutes were running, yet not daring the loss of time to look. " 'Tis not in consigning me to the enemy that you have your revenge on me, 'tis in making me vainly love you. I receive the greater hurt from your beauty, not from the British provost-marshal !"

" Bravado !" said she.

" Time will show," said he.

" If you are so strong a man that you can endure the one hurt so calmly, why are you not a little stronger, — strong enough to ignore this other hurt, — this *love*-wound, as you call it ?"

She blushed furiously, and much against her will, at the mere word, "love-wound." Her mood now seemed to be one of pretended incredulity, and yet of a vague unwillingness that the man should be so weak to her charms.

Peyton conceived that a change of play might aid his game.

" By heaven," he cried, " I will ! 'Tis a weakness, as you imply ! I shall close my heart, vanquish my feelings ! No word more of love ! I defy your beauty, your proud face, your splendid eyes ! I shall die free of your image. Go where you will, madam. It sha'n't be a puling lover that the British hang. A snap o' the finger for your all-conquering charms ! — why do you not leave me ?"

" What ! Do you order me from my own parlor ?"

Hope accelerated Peyton's heart at this, but he feigned indifference.

"Go or stay," he said; "'tis nothing to me!"

"You rebel, you speak like that to me!"

Her speech rang with genuine anger, and of a little hotter quality than he had thought to raise.

He was about to answer, when suddenly a sound, far and faint, reached his ear. "Isn't that — do you hear —" he said, huskily, and turning cold.

"Horses?" said Elizabeth. "Yes, — on the road from King's Bridge."

She went to one of the eastern windows, opened the sash, unfastened the shutter without, and let in a rush of cold air. Then she closed the sash and looked out through the small panes.

"Is it —" said Peyton, quietly, with as much steadiness as he could command, "I wonder — can it be —"

"A troop of rangers!" said Elizabeth. "And Sam is with them!" She closed the shutter, and turned to Peyton, her face still glowing with the resentment elicited by the cavalier attitude he had assumed before this alarm. "Go or stay, 'tis nothing to you, you said! The last insult, Sir Rebel Captain!" and she made for the door.

"You mustn't go! You mustn't go!" was the only speech he could summon. But she was already passing him. He snatched a kerchief from her dress,

and dropped it on the floor. She did not observe
his act. "Pardon me!" he cried. "Your kerchief!
You've dropped it, don't you see?"

She turned and saw it on the floor.

Peyton quickly stepped from behind his chair,
stooped and picked up the kerchief, kissed it, and
handed it to her, then staggered to his former support, showing in his face and by a groan the pain
caused him by his movement.

"Your wound!" said Elizabeth, standing still.
"You shouldn't have stooped!"

Harry's pain and consequent weakness, added to
his consciousness of the rapidly approaching enemy,
who had already turned in from the main road,
gave him a pallor that would have claimed the
attention of a less compassionate woman even than
Elizabeth.

"No matter!" he murmured, feebly. Then, as if
about to swoon, he threw his head back, lost his hold
of the chair-back, and staggered to the spinet. Leaning on this, he gasped, "My cravat! I feel as if I
were choking!" and made some futile effort with his
hand to unfasten the neck-cloth. "Would you," he
panted, "may I beg — loosen it?"

She went to his side, undid the cravat, and otherwise relieved his neck of its confinement. She could
not but meet his gaze as she did so. It was a gaze
of eager, adoring eyes. He feebly smiled his thanks,

and spoke, between short breaths, the words, "The hour — I love you — yes, the troops!"

The horses were clattering up towards the house.

A voice of command was heard through the window.

"Halt! Guard the windows and the rear, you four!"

"Colden's voice!" exclaimed Peyton.

Elizabeth was somewhat startled. "He must have been still at King's Bridge when Sam arrived," said she.

"He must be a close friend," said Peyton.

"He is my affianced husband."

Peyton staggered, as if shot, around the projection of the spinet, and came to a rest in the small space between that projection and the west wall of the room. "Her affianced! Then it's all up with me!"

The outside door was heard to open. Elizabeth turned her back towards the spinet and Peyton, and faced the door to the hall. That, too, was flung wide. Peyton dropped on his right knee, behind the spinet, leaning forward and stretching his wounded leg out behind him, just as Colden rushed in at the head of six of the Queen's Rangers, who were armed with short muskets. The major stopped short at sight of Elizabeth, and the rangers stood behind him, just within the door. Peyton was hidden by the spinet.

"Where is the rebel, Elizabeth?" cried Colden.

She met his gaze straight, and spoke calmly, with a barely perceptible tremor.

"You are too late, Jack! The prisoner has eluded me. Look for him on the road to Tarrytown, — and be quick about it, for God's sake!"

Colden drew back aghast, thrown from the height of triumph to the depth of chagrin. Peyton, fearing lest the one joyous bound of his heart might have betrayed him, remained perfectly still, knowing that if any movement should take Elizabeth from between the soldiers and the projection of the spinet, or if the soldiers should enter further and chance to look under the spinet, he would be seen.

"Don't you understand?" said Elizabeth, assuming one impatience to conceal another. "There's no time to lose! 'Twas the rebel Peyton! He's afoot!"

"The road to Tarrytown, you say?" replied Colden, gathering back his faculties.

"Yes, to Tarrytown! Why do you wait?" Her vehemence of tone sufficed to cover the growing insupportability of her situation.

"To the road again, men!" Colden ordered. "Till we meet, Elizabeth!" And he hastened, with the rangers, from the place.

Peyton and Elizabeth remained motionless till the sound of the horses was afar. Then Elizabeth called

"'YOU ARE TOO LATE, JACK!'"

Williams, who, as she had supposed, had come into the hall with the rangers. He now entered the parlor. Elizabeth, whose back was still towards Peyton, who had risen and was leaning on the spinet, addressed the steward in a low, embarrassed tone, as if ashamed of the weakness newly come over her.

" Williams, this gentleman will remain in the house till his wound is healed. His presence is to be a secret in the household. He will occupy the southwestern chamber." She then turned and spoke, in a constrained manner, to Peyton, not meeting his look. " It is the room your General Washington had when he was my father's guest."

With an effort, she raised her eyes to his, but shyly dropped them again. He bowed his thanks gravely, rather shamefaced at the success of his deception. A moment later, Elizabeth, with averted glance, walked quickly from the room.

CHAPTER VIII.

THE steward immediately set about preparing the designated chamber for occupancy, so that Peyton, on being carried up to it a few minutes later, found it warm and lighted. It was a large, square, panelled apartment, in which the fireplace of 1682 remained unchanged, a wide, deep, square opening, faced with Dutch tile, of which there were countless pieces, each piece having a picture of some Scriptural incident. Into this fireplace, where a log was burning crisply, Peyton gazed languidly as he lay on the bed, his clothes having been removed by black Sam, who had been assigned to attend him, and who now lay in the wide hall without. Williams had taken another look at the wound, and expressed a favorable opinion of its condition. A lighted candle was placed within Peyton's reach, on a table by the bedside. Williams had brought him, at Elizabeth's orders, part of what remained from the general supper. The captain felt decidedly comfortable.

He supposed that Colden, after abandoning the false chase, would make another call at the house, but he inferred from Elizabeth's previous conduct that she could and would send the Tory major and the rangers back to King's Bridge without opportunity of discovering her guest. And, indeed, Elizabeth had so provided. On returning to the dining-room from her fateful interview with Peyton, she had answered the astonished and inquisitive looks of Miss Sally and Mr. Valentine, by saying, in an abrupt and reserved manner, " For important reasons I have chosen not to give the prisoner up. He will stay in the house for a time, and nobody is to know he is here. Please remember, Mr. Valentine." The old man tried to recall Peyton's words in asking him to send Elizabeth to the parlor, and made a mental effort to put this and that together ; failing in which, he decided to repeat nothing of Peyton's conversation, lest it might in some way appear that he had "lent aid." He now lighted his lantern, and sallied forth on his long walk homeward over the wind-swept roads. Elizabeth, who, much to the dismay of her aunt's curiosity, had not broken silence save to give orders to the servants, now charged Williams to stay up till Colden should return, and to inform him that all were abed, that there was no news of the escaped prisoner, and that she desired the major to hasten to New York and relieve her family's anxiety. This command the steward executed about midnight, with the result that the

major, utterly tired out and sadly disappointed, rode
away from the manor-house a third time that night,
more disgruntled than on either of the two previous
occasions. By this time the house was dark and
silent, Elizabeth and her aunt having long retired,
the latter with a remark concerning the effect of late
hours on the complexion, a hope that Mr. Valentine
would not fall into a puddle on the way home, and
a curiosity as to how the rebel captain fared.

The rebel captain, afar in his spacious chamber,
was mentally in a state of felicity. As he ceased to
remember the conquered, abashed look Elizabeth's
face had last worn, he ceased to feel ashamed of
having deceived her. Her earlier manner recurred
to his mind, and he jubilated inwardly over having
got the better of this arrogant and vengeful young
creature. Even had she been otherwise, and had
his life depended on tricking her with a pretence
of love, he would have valued his life far above her
feelings, and would not have hesitated to practise
on her a falsehood that many a gentleman has
practised on many a maid for no higher purpose
than for the sport or for the testing of his powers,
and often for no other purpose than the maid's
undoing in more than her feelings. How much
less, then, need he consider her feelings when he
regarded her as an enemy in war, of whom it
was his right to take all possible advantage for

the saving of his own or any other American soldier's life! These thoughts came only at those moments when it occurred to him that his act might need justification. But if he thought he was entitled to avail himself of these excuses, he deceived himself, for no such considerations had been in his mind before or during his act. He had proceeded on the impulse of self-preservation alone, with no further thought as to the effect on her feelings than the hope that her feelings would be moved in his behalf. He had been totally selfish in the matter, and yet, while it is true he had not stopped to reason whether the act was morally justifiable or not, he had *felt* that her attitude warranted his deception, or, rather, he had not felt that the deception was a discreditable act, as he might have felt had her attitude been kindlier. Even had he possessed any previous scruples about that act, he would have overcome them. As it was, the scruples came only when he thought of that new, chastened, subdued look on her face. Only then did he feel that his trick might be debatable, as to whether it became a gentleman. Only then did he take the trouble to seek justifiable circumstances. Only then did he have a dim sense of what might be the feelings of a girl suddenly stormed into love. He had never been sufficiently in love to know how serious a feeling

—serious in its tremendous potency for joy or pain — love is. In Virginia, in London, and in Ireland, he had indulged himself in such little flirtations, such amours of an hour, as helped make up a young gentleman's amusements. But he had long been, as he was now, heart-free, and, though it occurred to him that, in this girl, so great a change of mien must arise from a pronounced change of heart, he had no thought that her new mood could have deep root or long life. So, less from what thoughts he did have on the subject than from his absence of thought thereon, he lapsed into peace of mind, and went to sleep, rejoicing in his security and trusting it would last. Her face did not appear in his dreams. He had not retained a strong or accurate impression of that face. His mind had been too full of other things, even while enacting his impromptu love-scene, to make note of her beauty. He had been sensible, of course, that she was beautiful, but there had not been time or circumstance for flirtation. He had not for an instant viewed her as a possible object of conquest for its own sake. She had been to him only an enemy, in the shape of a beautiful young girl, and of whom it had become necessary to make use. And so his dreams that night were made up of wild cavalry charges, rides through the wind, and painful crushings and tearings of his leg.

Elizabeth's thoughts were in a whirl, her feelings beyond analysis. She was sensible mainly of a wholly novel and vast pleasure at the adoration so impetuously expressed for her by this audacious stranger, of a pride in his masterful way, of applause for that very manner which she had rebuked as insolence. Was this love at last? Undoubtedly; for she had read all the romances and plays and poems, and, if this feeling of hers were a thing other than the love they all described, they would have described such a feeling also. Because she had never felt its soft touch before, she had thought herself exempt from it. But now that it had found lodgment in her, she knew it at once, from the very fact that in a flash she understood all the romances and plays and poems that had before interested her but as mere tales, whose motives had seemed arbitrary and insufficient. Now they all took reality and reason. She knew at last why Hero threw herself into the Hellespont after Leander, why all that commotion was caused by Helen of Troy, why Oriana took such trouble for Mirabel, why Juliet died on Romeo's body, why Miss Richland paid Honeywood's debts. The moon, rushing through a cleft in the clouds (she had opened one of the shutters on putting out the candles), had for her a sudden beauty which accounted for the fine things the poets had said of it and love together. Yes, because it opened

on her world of romance a magic window, letting in
a wondrous light, waking that world to throbbing
life, clothing it with indescribable charm, she knew
the name of the key that had unlocked her own
heart. Now she knew them all, — the heroes, the
fairy princes, the knights errant ; perceived that
they were real and live, recognized their traits and
manners, their very faces, in that bold, free, strong
young rebel ; he was Orlando, and Lovelace, and
Prince Charming, and Æneas, and Tom Jones, and
King Harry the Fifth, and young Marlowe, and even
Captain Macheath (she had read forbidden books
guilelessly, in course of reading everything at hand),
and Roderick Random, and Captain Plume, and all
the conquering, gallant, fine young fellows, at the
absurd weakness of whose sweethearts she had
marvelled beyond measure. She understood that
weakness now, and knew, too, why those sweethearts had, in the first delicious hours of their weakness, trembled and dropped their eyes before those
young gentlemen. For, as she mentally beheld his
image, she felt her own cheeks glow, and in imagination was fain to drop her own eyes before his bold,
unquailing look. She wondered, with confusion and
unseen blushes, how she would face him at their
next meeting, and felt that she must not, could not,
be the one to cause that meeting. Right surely had
this fair castle, that had withstood many a long siege,

fallen now at a single onslaught, and that but a sham onslaught. The haughty princess in her tower had not longed for the prince, but the prince had arrived, not to her rescue, but to the taming of her. And alas! the prince, whom she fondly thought her lover, was no more lover of her than of the picture of her female ancestor on his bedroom wall!

She gave no thought to consequences, and, as for Jack Colden, she simply, by power of will, kept him out of her mind.

It was three days before Peyton could walk about his room, and two days more before he felt sufficient confidence in his wounded leg to come down-stairs and take his meals with the household. And even then, refusing a crutch, he used a stick in moving about. During the five days when he kept his room, he was waited on alternately by Sam and Cuff, who served at his bath and brought his food; and occasionally Molly carried to him at dinner some belated delicacy or forgotten dish. Williams, too, visited him daily, and expressed a kind of professional satisfaction at the uninterrupted healing of the wound, which the steward treated with the mysterious applications known to home surgery. Williams lent his own clean linen to Harry, while Harry's underwent washing and mending at the hands of the maid. Old Valentine, who visited the house every day, the weather being cold and sometimes cloudy, but without rain, called at the sick chamber now and then, and filled it with tobacco smoke, homely philosophy, and rustic reminiscence. Harry had no other visitors. During these five days he saw not Elizabeth or Miss Sally, save from his window twice or thrice, at which times they were walking on the terrace. In daytime, when no artificial light was in the room to betray to some possible outsider the presence of a guest, he had the shutters opened of one of the two south windows and of one of the two west ones. Often he reclined near a window, pleasing his eyes with the view. Westward lay the terrace, the wide river, the leafy cliffs, and fair rolling country beyond. His eye could take in also the deer paddock, which the hand of war had robbed of its inmates, and the great orchard northward overlooking the river. Through the south window he could see the little branch road and boat-landing, the old stone mill, the winding Neperan and its broad mill-pond, and the sloping, ravine-cut, wooded stretch of country, between the post-road on the left and the deep-set Hudson on the right. The spire of St. John's Church, among the yew-trees, with the few edifices grouped near it, broke gratefully the deserted aspect of things, at the left. The spacious scene, so richly filled by nature, had in its loneliness and repose a singular sweetness. Rarely was any one abroad. Only when the Hessians or Loyalist dragoons patrolled the post-road, or when some British sloop-of-war showed its white sails far down the river, was there sign of human life and conflict. The deserted look of things was in harmony with the spirit of a book with which Harry sweetened the long hours of his recovery. It was a book that Elizabeth had sent up for his amusement, called " The Man of Feeling," and there was something in the opening picture of the venerable mansion, with its air of melancholy, its languid stillness, its " single crow, perched on an old tree by the side of the gate," and its young lady passing between the trees with a book in her hand, that harmonized with his own sequestered state. He liked the tale better than the same author's later novel, " The Man of the World," which he had read a few years before. Every day he inquired about his hostess's health, and sent his compliments and thanks. He was glad she did not visit him in person, for such a visit might involve an allusion to their last previous interview, and he did not know in what manner he should make or treat such allusion. He felt it would be an awkward matter to get out of the situation of pretended adorer, and he was for putting that awkward matter off till the last possible moment.

It was necessary for him to think of his return to the army. Duty and inclination required he should make that return as soon as could be. His first impulse had been to send word of his whereabouts and condition. But as Elizabeth had not offered a messenger, he was loath to ask for one. Moreover, the messenger might be intercepted by the enemy's patrols and induced by fear to betray the message. Then, too, even if the messenger should reach the American lines uncaught, a consequent attempt to convey a wounded man from the manor hall to the camp might attract the attention of the vigilant patrols, and risk not only Harry's own recapture, but also the loss of other men. Decidedly, the best course was to await the healing of his wound, and then to make his way alone, under cover of night, to the army. He knew that, whatever might occur, it was now Elizabeth's interest to protect him, for should she give him up, the disclosure that she had formerly shielded him would render her liable to suspicion and ridicule. He felt, too, from the manifestations he had seen of her will and of her ingenuity, that she was quite able to protect him. So he rested in security in the quiet old chamber, dreading only the task of taking back his love-making. Of that task, the difficulty would depend on Elizabeth's own conduct, which he could not foresee, and that in turn on her state of heart, which he did not exactly divine. He knew only that she had, in that critical moment of the troops' arrival, felt for him a tenderness that betokened love. Whether that feeling had flourished or declined, he could not, during the five days when they did not meet, be aware.

It had not declined. She had gone on idealizing the confident rebel captain all the while. The fact that he was of the enemy added piquancy to the sentiments his image aroused. It lent, too, an additional poetic interest to the idea of their love. Was not Romeo of the enemies of Juliet's house? The fact of her being now his protector, by its oppositeness to the conventional situation, gave to their relation the charm of novelty, and also gratified her natural love of independence and domination. Yet that very love, in a woman, may afford its owner keen delight by receiving quick and confident opposition and conquest from a man, and such Elizabeth's had received from Peyton, both in the matter of the horse and in that of his successful wooing. But the greater her softness for him, the greater was her delicacy regarding him, and the more in conformity with the strictest propriety must be her conduct towards him. Her pride demanded this tribute of her love, in compensation for the latter's immense exactions on the former in the sudden yielding to his wooing. Moreover, she would not appear in anything short of perfection in his eyes. She would not make her company cheap to him. If she had been a quick conquest, up to the point of her first token of submission, she would be all the slower in

the subsequent stages, so that the complete yielding
should be no easier than ought to be that of one
valued as she would have him value her.   All this
she felt rather than thought, and she acted on it
punctiliously.

She did not confide in her aunt, though that lady
watched her closely and had her suspicions.   Yet
there was apparent so little warrant for these suspicions, save the protection of the rebel in itself, that
Miss Sally often imagined Elizabeth had other reasons, reasons of policy, for the sudden change of
intention that had resulted in that protection.   Elizabeth's conduct was always so mystifying to everybody!
And when this thought possessed Miss Sally, she
underwent a pleasing agitation, which she in turn
kept secret, and which attended the hope that perhaps the handsome captain might not be averse to
her conversation.   She had both read and observed
that the taste of youth sometimes was for ripeness.
She might atone, in a measure, for Elizabeth's disdain.   She would have liked to visit him daily, with
condolence and comfortings, but she could not do
so without previous sanction of the mistress of the
house, which sanction Elizabeth briefly but very
peremptorily refused.   Miss Sally thought it a cruelty that the prisoner should be deprived of what
consolation her society might afford, and dwelt on
this opinion until she became convinced he was

actually pining for her presence. This made her poutish and reproachfully silent to Elizabeth, and sighful and whimsical to herself. The slightly strained feeling that arose between aunt and niece was quite acceptable to Elizabeth, as it gave her freedom for her own dreams, and prohibited any occasion for an expression of feelings or opinions of her own as to the captain. But Miss Sally's symptoms were observed by old Mr. Valentine, who, inferring their cause, underwent much unrest on account of them, became snappish and sarcastic towards the lady, watchful both of her and of Peyton, and moody towards the others in the house. It was the old man's disquietude regarding the state of Miss Sally's affections that brought him to the house every day. For one brief while he considered the advisability of transferring his attentions back from Miss Sally to the widow Babcock, who had possessed them first, but, when he tarried in the parsonage, his fears as to what might be going on in the manor-house made his stay in the former intolerable, and led him irresistibly to the latter.

Meanwhile the wounded guest, so unconscious of the states of mind caused by him in the household, was the evoker of flutters in yet another female breast. The girl, Molly, had read toilsomely through "Pamela," and saw no reason why an equally attractive housemaid should not aspire to an equally high destiny on this side of the ocean. But, often as she artfully contrived that the black boy should forget some part of the guest's dinner, and timely as she planned her own visits with the missing portion, she found the officer heedless of her smiles, engrossed sometimes in his meal, sometimes in his book, sometimes in both. She conceived a loathing for that book, more than once resisted a temptation to make way with it, and, having one day stolen a look into it, thenceforth abominated the poor young lady of it, with all the undying bitterness of an unpreferred rival.

Though Elizabeth and her aunt found each other reticent, they yet passed their time together, breakfasting early, then visiting the widow Babcock or some tenant, dining at noon, spending the early afternoon, the one at her book or embroidery, the other in a siesta before the fireplace, supping early, then preparing for the night by a brisk walk in the garden, or on the terrace, or to the orchard and back. Elizabeth had Williams provided with instructions as to his conduct in the event of a visit from King's troops, and, to make Peyton's security still less uncertain, she confined her walks to the immediate vicinity. The house itself was kept in a pretence of being closed, the shutters of the parlor being skilfully adjusted to admit light, and yet, from the road, appear fast.

Thus Elizabeth, finding enjoyment in the very look and atmosphere of the old house, fulfilled quietly the purpose of her capricious visit, and at the same time cherished a dreamy pleasure such as she had not thought of finding in that visit.

On the fifth day after Peyton's arrival, Williams announced that the captain would venture downstairs on the morrow. The next morning Elizabeth waited in the east parlor to receive him. Whatever inward excitement she underwent, she was on the surface serene. She was dressed in her simplest, having purposely avoided any appearance of desiring to appear at her best. Her aunt, who stood with her, on the other side of the fireplace, was perceptibly flustered, being got up for the occasion, with ribbons in evidence and smiles ready for production on the instant. When the west door opened, and the awaited hero entered, pale but well groomed, using his cane in such fashion that he could carry himself erectly, Elizabeth greeted him with formal courtesy. Though her manner had the repose necessary to conceal her sweet agitation, an observant person might have noticed a deference, a kind of meekness, that was new in her demeanor towards men. Peyton, whose mien (though not his feeling) was a reflex of her own, was relieved at this appearance of indifference, and hoped it would continue. His mind being on this, the stately curtsey and profuse smirks of Miss Sally were quite lost on him.

The three breakfasted together in the dining-room, a large and cheerful apartment whose front windows, looking on the lawn, were the middle features of the eastern façade of the house. The mass of decorative woodwork, and the fireplace in the north side of the room, added to its impression of comfort as well as to its beauty. Conversation at the breakfast was ceremonious and on the most indifferent subjects, despite the attempts of Miss Sally, who would have monopolized Peyton's attention, to inject a little cordial levity. After breakfast Elizabeth, to avoid the appearance of distinguishing the day, took her aunt off for the usual walk, which she purposely prolonged to unusual length, much to Miss Sally's annoyance. Peyton passed the morning in reading a new play that had made great talk in London the year before, namely, "The School for Scandal." It was one of the new books received by Colonel Philipse from London, by a recent English vessel, — plays being, in those days, good enough to be much read in book form, — and brought out from town by Elizabeth. The dinner was, as to the attitude of the participants towards one another, a repetition of the breakfast. In the afternoon, Peyton having expressed an intention of venturing outdoors for a little air, Elizabeth assigned Sam to attend him, and said that, as he had to traverse the south hall and stairs in going to his room, he might thereafter put to his own service the unused south door in leaving and entering the house. Harry strolled for a few minutes on the terrace, but his lameness made walking little pleasure, and he returned to the east parlor, where Elizabeth sat reading while her aunt was looking drowsily at the fire. Peyton took a chair at the right side of the fireplace, and mentally contrasted his present security with his peril in that place on a former occasion.

The trampling of horses at a distance elicited from Elizabeth the words, "The Hessian patrol, on the Albany road, as usual, I suppose." But, the clatter increasing, she arose and looked through the narrow slit whereby light was admitted between the almost closed shutters. After a moment she said, in unconcealed alarm :

"Oh, heaven! 'Tis a party of Lord Cathcart's officers! They said at King's Bridge they'd come one day to pay their respects. How can I keep them out?"

Peyton arose, but remained by the fireplace, and said, "To keep them out, if they think themselves expected, would excite suspicion. I will go to my room."

Elizabeth, meanwhile, had opened the window to

draw the shutter close; but her trembling movement, assisted by a passing breeze, and by the
perversity of inanimate things, caused the shutter
to fly wide open.

She turned towards Peyton, with signs of fright
on her face. "Back!" she whispered. "They'll
see you through the window. Into the closet, —
the closet!" She motioned imperatively towards
the pair of doors immediately beside him, west
of the fireplace. Hearing the horses' footfalls near
at hand, and perceiving, with her, that he would
not have time to walk safely across the parlor to
the hall, he opened one of the doors indicated by
her, and stepped into the closet.

In the instant before he closed the door after him,
he noticed the stairs descending backward from the
right side of the closet. He foresaw that the British
officers would come into the parlor. If they should
make a long stay, he might have to change his position during their presence. He might thus cause
sufficient sound to attract attention. He would be
in better case further away. Therefore, using his
stick and feeling the route with his hand, he made
his way down the steps to a landing, turned to the
right, descended more steps, and found himself in
a dark cellar. He had no sooner reached the last
step than a burst of hearty greetings from above
informed him the officers were in the parlor.

This part of the cellar being damp, he set out in search of a more comfortable spot wherein to bestow himself the necessary while. Groping his way, and travelling with great labor, he at last came into a kind of corridor formed between two rolls of piled-up barrels. He proceeded along this passage until it was blocked by a barrel on the ground. On this he sat down, deciding it as good a staying-place as he might find. Leaning back, he discovered with his head what seemed to be a thick wooden partition close to the barrel. Changing his position, he bumped his head against an iron something that lay horizontally against the partition, and so violent was this collision that the iron something was moved from its place, a fact which he noted on the instant but immediately forgot in the sharpness of his pain.

Having at last made himself comfortable, he sat waiting in the darkness, thinking to let some time pass before returning to the closet stairway. An hour or more had gone by, when he heard a door open, which he knew must be at the head of some other stairway to the cellar, and a jocund voice cry: "Damme, we'll be our own tapsters! Give me the candle, Mr. Williams, and if my nose doesn't pull me to the barrel in one minute, may it never whiff spirits again!" A moment later, quick footfalls sounded on the stairs, then candle-light disturbed the blackness, and Williams was heard saying, "This way, gentlemen, if you insist. The barrel is on the ground, straight ahead." Whereupon Peyton saw two merry young Englishmen enter the very passage at whose end he sat, one bearing the candle, both followed by the steward, who carried a spigot and a huge jug.

Harry instantly divined the cause of this intrusion. The servants were busy preparing refreshments for the officers, and, in a spirit of gaiety, these two had volunteered to help Williams fetch the liquor which he, not knowing Harry's whereabouts, was about to draw from the barrel on which Harry sat.

It was not Elizabeth who could save him from discovery now.

The officers came groping towards him up the narrow passage.

Before the candle-light reached him, he rose and got behind the barrel, there being barely room for his legs between it and the partition. He had, in dressing for the day, put on his scabbard and his broken sword. He now took his stick in his left hand, and drew his sword with his right. He set his teeth hard together, thought of nothing at all, or rather of everything at once, and waited.

"Hear the rats," said one of the Englishmen. It was Peyton's stealthy movement he had heard.

"Ay, sir, there's often a terrible scampering of 'em," said Williams.

"Maybe I can pink a rat or two," said the officer without the candle, and drew his sword. Harry braced himself rapidly against the woodwork at his back. The candle-light touched the barrel.

At that instant Harry felt the woodwork give way behind him, and fell on his back on the ground.

"What's that?" cried the officer with the candle, standing still.

"'Tis the scampering of the rats, of course," said the other.

Harry had apprehended, by this time, that the supposed wooden partition was in reality a door in the cellar wall. He now pushed it shut with his foot, remaining outside of it, then rose, and, feeling about him, discovered that his present place was in a narrow arched passage that ran, from the door in the cellar wall, he knew not how far. Recalling the bumping of his head, he inferred now that the iron something was a bolt, and that his blow had forced it from its too large socket in the stone wall.

He proceeded onward in the dark passage for some distance, then stopped to listen. No sound coming from the door he had closed, he decided that the officers were satisfied the noise had been of the rats' making. He sheathed his broken sword, having retained that and his stick in his fall, and went forward, hoping to find a habitable place of waiting. Soon the passage widened into a kind of subterranean

room, one side of which admitted light. Going to
this side, Harry stopped short at the verge of a well,
on whose circumference the subterranean chamber
abutted. The light came from the well's top, which
was about ten feet above the low roof of the underground room, the passage from the cellar being
on a descent. In this artificial cave were wooden
chests, casks, and covered earthen vessels, these contents proclaiming the place a secret storage-room
designed for use in siege or in military occupation.
Harry waited here a while that seemed half a day,
then returned through the passage to the door, intending to return to the cellar. He listened at the
door, found all quiet beyond, and made to push open
the door. It would not move. From the feel of
the resistance, he perceived that the bolt had been
pushed home again — as indeed it had, by the steward, who had noticed it while tapping the barrel, and
had imputed its being drawn to some former care-
lessness of his own.

Peyton, finding himself thus barred into the subterranean regions, was in a quandary. Any alarm
he might attempt, by shouting or pounding, might
not be heard, or, if heard, might reach some tarrying
British. In due time, Elizabeth would doubtless
have him looked for in the closet and then in the
cellar, but, on his not being found there, would suppose he had left the cellar by one of the other stair-

ways. Thus he could little hope to be sought for in his prison. Williams might at any time have occasion to visit the secret storeroom, but, on the other hand, he might not have such occasion for weeks. Harry groped back to the cave, and sought some way of escape by the well, but found none.

He then examined the cave more closely, and came finally on another passage than that by which he had entered. He followed this for what seemed an interminable length. At last, it closed up in front of him. He tested the barrier of raw earth with his hands, felt a great round stone projecting therefrom, pushed this stone in vain, then clasped it with both arms and pulled. It gave, and presently fell to the ground at his feet, leaving an aperture two feet across, which let in light. He crawled the short length of this, and breathed the open air in a small thicket on the sloping bank of the Hudson.[8] He crept to the thicket's edge, and saw, in the sunset light, the river before him ; on the river, a British war-vessel ; on the vessel, some naval officers, one of whom was looking, with languid preoccupation, straight at the thicket from which Harry gazed.

CHAPTER IX.

THE CONFESSION.

"What d'ye spy, Tom?" called out another officer on the deck, to the one whose attitude most
interested Harry.

"I thought I made out some kind of craft steering
through the bushes yonder," was the answer.

"I see nothing."

"Neither do I, now. 'Twasn't human craft, anyhow, so it doesn't signify," and the officers looked
elsewhere.

Harry lay low in the thicket, awaiting the departure of the vessel or the arrival of darkness. On
the deck there was no sign of weighing anchor.
As night came, the vessel's lights were slung. The
sky was partly clear in the west, and stars appeared in that direction, but the east was overcast,
so that the rising moon was hid. The atmosphere
grew colder.

When Harry could make out nothing of the vessel
on the dark water, save the lights that glowed like
low-placed stars, he crawled from the bushes and up

the bank to the terrace. He then rose and proceeded, with the aid of his stick, aching from having so long maintained a cramped position, and from the suddenly increased cold. Before him, as he continued to ascend, rose the house, darkness outlined against darkness. No sound came from it, no window was lighted. This meant that the British officers had left, for their presence would have been marked by plenitude of light and by noise of merriment. Harry stopped on the terrace, and stood in doubt how to proceed. What had been thought of his disappearance? Where would he be supposed to have gone? Had provision been made for his possible return? Perhaps he should find a guiding light in some window on the other side of the house; perhaps a servant remained alert for his knock on the door. His only course was to investigate, unless he would undergo a night of much discomfort.

As he was about to approach the house, he was checked by a sight so vaguely outlined that it might be rather of his imagination than of reality, and which added a momentary shiver of a keener sort than he already underwent from the weather. A dark cloaked and hooded figure stood by the balustrade that ran along the roof-top. As Peyton looked, his hand involuntarily clasping his sword-hilt, and the stories of the ghosts that haunted this old mansion shot through his mind, the figure seemed to descend through the very roof, as a stage ghost is lowered through a trap. He continued to stare at the spot where it had stood, but nothing reappeared against the backing of black cloud. Wondering much, Harry presently went on towards the house, turned the southwest corner, and skirted the south front as far as to the little porch in its middle. Intending to reconnoitre all sides of the house before he should try one of the doors, he was passing on, after a glance at the south door lost in the blacker shadows of the porch, when suddenly the fan-window over the door seemed to glow dimly with a wavering light. He placed his hand on one of the Grecian pillars of the porch, and watched. A moment later the door softly opened. A figure appeared, beyond the threshold, bearing a candle. The figure wore a cloak with a hood, but the hood was down.

"All is safe," whispered a low voice. "The officers went hours ago. I knew you must have escaped from the house, and were hiding somewhere. I saw you a minute ago from the roof gallery."

Peyton having entered, Elizabeth swiftly closed and locked the door behind him, handed him the candle with a low "Good night," and fled silently, ghostlike, up the stairs, disappearing quickly in the darkness.

Harry made his way to his own room, as in a kind of dream. She herself had waited and watched for him! This, then, was the effect wrought in the proudest, most disdainful young creature of her sex, by that feeling which he had, by telling and acting a lie, awakened in her. The revelation set him thinking. How long might such a feeling last? What would be its effect on her after his departure? He had read, and heard, and seen, that, when these feelings were left to pine away slowly, the people possessing them pined also. And this was the return he was about to give his most hospitable hostess, the woman who had saved his life! Yet what was to be done? His life belonged to his country, his chosen career was war; he could not alter completely his destiny to save a woman some pining. After all, she *would* get over it; yet it would make of her another woman, embitter her, change entirely the complexion of the world to her, and her own attitude towards it. He tried to comfort himself with the thought of her engagement to Colden, of which he had not learned until after the mischief had been done. But he recalled her manner towards Colden, and a remark of old Mr. Valentine's, whence he knew that the engagement was not, on her side, a love one, and was not inviolable. Yet it would be a crime to a woman of her pride, of her power of loving, to allow the deceit, his pretence of love, to go as far as marriage. A disclosure would come in time, and would bring her a bitter awakening. The falsehood, natural if not excusable in its circumstances, and broached without thought of ultimate consequence, must be stopped at once.   He must leave her presence immediately, but, before going, must declare the truth.   She must not be allowed to waste another day of her life on an illusion.   Aside from the effect on her heart, of the continuance of the delusion, it would doubtless affect her outward circumstances, by leading her to break her engagement with Colden.   An immediate discovery of the truth, moreover, by creating such a revulsion of feeling as would make her hate him, would leave her heart in a state for speedy healing.   This disclosure would be a devilishly unpleasant thing to make, but a soldier and a gentleman must meet unpleasant duties unflinchingly.

He lay a long time awake, disturbed by thoughts of the task before him.   When he did sleep, it was to dream that the task was in progress, then that it was finished but had to be begun anew, then that countless obstacles arose in succession to hinder him in it.   Dawn found him little refreshed in mind, but none the worse in body.   He found, on arising, that he could walk without aid from the stick, and he required no help in dressing himself.   Looking towards the river, he saw the British vessel heading for New York.   But that sight gave him little comfort, thanks to the ordeal before him, in contemplating which he neglected to put on his sword and scabbard, and so descended to breakfast without them.

That meal offered no opportunity for the disclosure, the aunt being present throughout. Immediately after breakfast, the two ladies went for their customary walk. While they were breasting the wind, between two rows of box in the garden, Miss Sally spoke of Major Colden's intention to return for Elizabeth at the end of a week, and said, "'Twill be a week this evening since you arrived. Is he to come for you to-day or to-morrow?"

"I don't know," said Elizabeth, shortly.

"But, my dear, you haven't prepared —"

"I sha'n't go back to-day, that is certain. If Colden comes before to-morrow, he can wait for me, — or I may send him back without me, and stay as long as I wish."

"But he will meet Captain Peyton —"

"It can be easily arranged to keep him from knowing Captain Peyton is here. I shall look to that."

Miss Sally sighed at the futility of her inquisitorial fishing. Not knowing Elizabeth's reason for saving the rebel captain, she had once or twice thought that the girl, in some inscrutable whim, intended to deliver him up, after all. She had tried frequently to fathom her niece's purposes, but had never got any satisfaction.

"I suppose," she went on, desperately, "if you go back to town, you will leave the captain in Williams's charge."

"If I go back before the captain leaves," said Elizabeth, thereby dashing her amiable aunt's secretly cherished hope of affording the wounded officer the pleasure of her own unalloyed society.

Elizabeth really did not know what she would do. Her actions, on Colden's return, would depend on the prior actions of the captain. No one had spoken to Peyton of her intention to leave after a week's stay. She had thought such an announcement to him from her might seem to imply a hint that it was time he should resume his wooing. That he would resume it, in due course, she took for granted. Measuring his supposed feelings by her own real ones, she assumed that her loveless betrothal to another would not deter Peyton's further courtship. She believed he had divined the nature of that betrothal. Nor would he be hindered by the prospect of their being parted some while by the war. Engagements were broken, wars did not last forever, those who loved each other found ways to meet. So he would surely speak, before their parting, of what, since it filled her heart, must of course fill his. But she would show no forwardness in the matter. She therefore avoided him till dinner-time.

At the table he abruptly announced that, as duty

required he should rejoin the army at the first moment possible, and as he now felt capable of making the journey, he would depart that night.

Miss Sally hid her startled emotions behind a glass of madeira, into which she coughed, chokingly. Molly, the maid, stopped short in her passage from the kitchen door to the table, and nearly dropped the pudding she was carrying. Elizabeth concealed her feelings, and told herself that his declaration must soon be forthcoming. She left it to him to contrive the necessary private interview.

After dinner, he sat with the ladies before the fire in the east parlor, awaiting his opportunity with much hidden perturbation. Elizabeth feigned to read. At last, habit prevailing, her aunt fell asleep. Peyton hummed and hemmed, looked into the fire, made two or three strenuous swallows of nothing, and opened his mouth to speak. At that instant old Mr. Valentine came in, newly arrived from the Hill, and "whew"-ing at the cold. Peyton felt like one for whom a brief reprieve had been sent by heaven.

All afternoon Mr. Valentine chattered of weather and news and old times. Peyton's feeling of relief was short-lasting ; it was supplanted by a mighty regret that he had not been permitted to get the thing over. No second opportunity came of itself, nor could Peyton, who found his ingenuity for once quite paralyzed, force one. Supper was announced, and was partaken of by Harry, in fidgety abstraction; by Elizabeth, in expectant but outwardly placid silence; by Miss Sally, in futile smiling attempts to make something out of her last conversational chances with the handsome officer; and by Mr. Valentine, in sedulous attention to his appetite, which still had the vigor of youth.

Almost as soon as the ladies had gone from the dining-room, Peyton rose and left the octogenarian in sole possession. In the parlor Harry found no one but Molly, who was lighting the candles.

"What, Molly?" said he, feeling more and more nervous, and thinking to retain, by constant use of his voice, a good command of it for the dreaded interview. "The ladies not here? They left Mr. Valentine and me at the supper-table."

"They are walking in the garden, sir. Miss Elizabeth likes to take the air every evening."

"'Tis a chill air she takes this evening, I'm thinking," he said, standing before the fire and holding out his hands over the crackling logs.

"A chill night for your journey," replied Molly. "I should think you'd wait for day, to travel."

Peyton, unobservant of the wistful sigh by which the maid's speech was accompanied, replied, "Nay, for me, 'tis safest travelling at night. I must go through dangerous country to reach our lines."

"It mayn't be as cold to-morrow night," persisted Molly.

" My wound is well enough for me to go now."

" 'Twill be better still to-morrow."

But Peyton, deep in his own preoccupation, neither deduced aught from the drift of her remarks nor saw the tender glances which attended them. While he was making some insignificant answer, the maid, in moving the candelabrum on the spinet, accidentally brushed therefrom his hat, which had been lying on it. She picked it up, in great confusion, and asked his pardon.

" 'Twas my fault in laying it there," said he, receiving it from her. " I'm careless with my things. I make no doubt, since I've been here, I've more than once given your mistress cause to wish me elsewhere."

" La, sir," said Molly, " I don't think — *any* one would wish you elsewhere ! " Whereupon she left the room, abashed at her own audacity.

" The devil ! " thought Peyton. " I should feel better if some one did wish me elsewhere."

As he continued gazing into the fire, and his task loomed more and more disagreeably before him, he suddenly bethought him that Elizabeth, in taking her evening walk, showed no disposition for a private meeting. Dwelling on that one circumstance, he thought for awhile he might have been wrong in supposing she loved him. But then the previous night's incident recurred to his mind. Nothing short of love could have induced such solicitude. But, then, as she sought no last interview, might he not be warranted in going away and leaving the disclosure to come gradually, implied by the absence of further word from him ? Yet, she might be purposely avoiding the appearance of seeking an interview. The reasons calling for a prompt confession came back to him. While he was wavering between one dictate and another, in came Mr. Valentine, with a tobacco pipe.

Like an inspiration, rose the idea of consulting the octogenarian. A man who cannot make up his own mind is justified in seeking counsel. Elizabeth could suffer no harm through Peyton's confiding in this sage old man, who was devoted to her and to her family. Mr. Valentine's very words on entering, which alluded to Peyton's pleasant visit as Elizabeth's guest, gave an opening for the subject concerned. A very few speeches led up to the matter, which Harry broached, after announcing that he took the old man for one experienced in matters of the heart, and receiving the admission that the old man *had* enjoyed a share of the smiles of the sex. But if the captain had thought, in seeking advice, to find reason for avoiding his ugly task, he was disappointed. Old Valentine, though he had for some days feared a possible state of things between the captain and Miss Sally, had observed Elizabeth, and his vast experience had enabled him to interpret symptoms to which others had been blind. "She has acted towards you," he said to Peyton, "as she never acted towards another man. She's shown you a meekness, sir, a kind of timidity." And he agreed that, if Peyton should go away without an explanation, it would make her throw aside other expectations, and would, in the end, "cut her to the heart." Valentine hinted at regrettable things that had ensued from a jilting of which himself had once been guilty, and urged on Peyton an immediate unbosoming, adding, "She'll be so took aback and so full of wrath at you, she won't mind the loss of you. She'll abominate you and get over it at once."

The idea came to Peyton of making the confession by letter, but this he promptly rejected as a coward's dodge. "It's a damned unpleasant duty, but that's the more reason I should face it myself."

At that moment the front door of the east hall was heard to open.

"It's Miss Elizabeth and her aunt," said Valentine, listening at the door.

"Then I'll have the thing over at once, and be gone! Mr. Valentine, a last kindness, — keep the aunt out of the room."

Before Valentine could answer, the ladies entered,

their cheeks reddened by the weather. Elizabeth carried a small bunch of belated autumn flowers.

"Well, I'm glad to come in out of the cold!" burst out Miss Sally, with a retrospective shudder. "Mr. Peyton, you've a bitter night for your going." She stood before the fire and smiled sympathetically at the captain.

But Peyton was heedful of none but Elizabeth, who had laid her flowers on the spinet and was taking off her cloak. Peyton quickly, with an "Allow me, Miss Philipse," relieved her of the wrap, which in his abstraction he retained over his left arm while he continued to hold his hat in his other hand. After receiving a word of thanks, he added, "You've been gathering flowers," and stood before her in much embarrassment.

"The last of the year, I think," said she. "The wind would have torn them off, if aunt Sally and I had not." And she took them up from the spinet to breath their odor.

Meanwhile Mr. Valentine had been whispering to Miss Sally at the fireplace. As a result of his communications, whatever they were, the aunt first looked doubtful, then cast a wistful glance at Peyton, and then quietly left the room, followed by the old man, who carefully closed the door after him.

While Elizabeth held the flowers to her nostrils, Peyton continued to stand looking at her, during an awkward pause. At length she replaced the nosegay on the spinet, and went to the fireplace, where she gazed at the writhing flames, and waited for him to speak.

Still laden with the cloak and hat, he desperately began :

"Miss Philipse, I — ahem — before I start on my walk to-night —"

"Your walk ?" she said, in slight surprise.

"Yes, — back to our lines, above."

"But you are not going to *walk* back," she said, in a low tone. "You are to have the horse, Cato."

Peyton stood startled. In a few moments he gulped down his feelings, and stammered :

"Oh — indeed — Miss Philipse — I cannot think of depriving you — especially after the circumstances."

She replied, with a gentle smile :

"You took the horse when I refused him to you. Now will you not have him when I offer him to you? You must, captain ! I'll not have so fine a horse go begging for a master. I'll not hear of your walking. On such a night, such a distance, through such a country !"

"The devil !" thought Harry. "This makes it ten times harder !"

Elizabeth now turned to face him directly. "Does not my cloak incommode you ?" she said, amusedly. "You may put it down."

"Oh, thank you, yes!" he said, feeling very red, and went to lay the cloak on the table, but in his confusion put down his own hat there, and kept the cloak over his arm. He then met her look recklessly, and blurted out:

"The truth is, Miss Philipse, now that I am soon to leave, I have something to — to say to you." His boldness here forsook him, and he paused.

"I know it," said Elizabeth, serenely, repressing all outward sign of her heart's blissful agitation.

"You do?" quoth he, astonished.

"Certainly," she answered, simply. "How could you leave without saying it?"

Peyton had a moment's puzzlement. Then, "Without saying what?" he asked.

"What you have to say," she replied, blushing, and lowering her eyes.

"But what have I to say?" he persisted.

She was silent a moment, then saw that she must help him out.

"Don't you know? You were not at all tongue-tied when you said it the evening you came here."

Peyton felt a gulf opening before him. "Good heaven," thought he, "she actually believes I am about to propose!"

Now, or never, was the time for the plunge. He drew a full breath, and braced himself to make it.

"But — ah — you see," said he, "the trouble is, —

what I said then is not what I have to say now.
You must understand, Miss Philipse, that I am
devoted to a soldier's career. All my time, all my
heart, my very life, belong to the service. Thus I
am, in a manner, bound no less on my side, than
you — I beg your pardon — "

"What do you mean?" She spoke quietly, yet
was the picture of open-eyed astonishment.

"Cannot you see?" he faltered.

"You mean" — her tone acquired resentment as
her words came — "that I, too, am bound on *my*
side, — to Mr. Colden?"

"I did not say so," he replied, abashed, cursing
his heedless tongue. He would not, for much, have
reminded her of any duty on her part.

She regarded him for a moment in silence, while
the clouds of indignation gathered. Then the storm
broke.

"You poltroon, I *do* see! You wish to take back
your declaration, because you are afraid of Colden's
vengeance!"

"Afraid? I afraid?" he echoed, mildly, surprised
almost out of his voice at this unexpected inference.

"Yes, you craven!" she cried, and seemed to
tower above her common height, as she stood erect,
tearless, fiery-eyed, and clarion-voiced. "Your cowardice outweighs your love! Go from my sight and
from my father's house, you cautious lover, with

your prudent scruples about the rights of your rival! Heavens, that I should have listened to such a coward! Go, I say! Spend no more time under this roof than you need to get your belongings from your room. Don't stop for farewells! Nobody wants them! Go,—and I'll thank you to leave my cloak behind you!"

Silenced and confounded by the force of her denunciation, he stupidly dropped the cloak to the floor where he stood, and stumbled from the room, as if swept away by the torrent of her wrath and scorn.

CHAPTER X.

THE PLAN OF RETALIATION.

It was in the south hall that he found himself,
having fled through the west door of the parlor, forgetful that his hat still remained on the table. He
naturally continued his retreat up the stairs to his
chamber. The only belongings that he had to get
there were his broken sword, his scabbard, and belt.
These he promptly buckled on, resolved to leave the
house forthwith.

Still tingling from the blow of her words, he yet
felt a great relief that the task was so soon over,
and that her speedy action had spared him the labor
of the long explanation he had thought to make.
As matters stood, they could not be improved. Her
love had turned to hate, in the twinkling of an eye.

And yet, how preposterously she had accounted
for his conduct! Dwelling on his hint, though it
was checked at its utterance, that she was already
bound, she had assumed that he held out her engagement to Colden as a barrier to their love. And
she believed, or pretended to believe, that his regard

for that barrier arose from fear of inviting a rival's
vengeance! As if he, who daily risked his life,
could fear the vengeance of a man whom he had
already once defeated with the sword! It was like
a woman to alight first on the most absurd possibility
the situation could imply. And if she knew the
conjecture was absurd, she was the more guilty of
affront in crying it out against him. He, in turn,
was now moved to anger. He would not have false
motives imputed to him. It would be useless to
talk to her while her present mood continued. But
he could write, and leave the letter where it would
be found. Inasmuch as he had faced the worst
storm his disclosure could have aroused, there was
no cowardice in resorting to a letter with such expla-
nations as could not be brought to her mind in any
other form. Two days previously, he had requested
writing materials in his room, for the sketching of
a report of his being wounded, and these were still
on a table by the window. He lighted candles, and
sat down to write.

When he had finished his document, sealed and
addressed it, he laid it on the table, where it would
attract the eye of a servant, and looked around for
his hat. Presently he recalled that he had left it in
the parlor. He first thought of seeking a servant,
and sending for it, lest he might meet Elizabeth,
should he again enter the parlor. But it would be

better to face her, for a moment, than to give an order to a servant of a house whence he had been ordered out. And now, as he intended to go into the parlor, he would preferably leave the letter in that room, where it would perhaps reach her own eyes before any other's could fall on it. He therefore took up the letter, thrust it for the time in his belt, descended quietly to the south hall, cautiously opened the parlor door, peeped through the crack, saw with relief that only Miss Sally was in the room, threw the door wide, and strode quickly towards the table on which he thought he had left his hat.

But, as he approached, he saw that the hat was not there.

In the meantime, during the few minutes he had spent in his room, things had been occurring in this parlor. As soon as Peyton had left it, or had been carried out of it by the resistless current of Elizabeth's invective, the girl had turned her anger on herself, for having weakened to this man, made him her hero, indulged in those dreams! She could scarcely contain herself. Having mechanically picked up her cloak, where Peyton had let it fall, she evinced a sudden unendurable sense of her humiliation and folly, by hurling the cloak with violence across the room. At that moment old Mr. Valentine entered, placidly seeking his pipe, which he had left behind him.

The octogenarian looked surprisedly at the cloak, then at Elizabeth, then mildly asked her if she had seen his pipe.

"Oh, the cowardly wretch!" was Elizabeth's answer, her feelings forcing a release in speech.

"What, me?" asked the old man, startled, not yet having thought to connect her words with his last interview with the American officer. He looked at her for a moment, but, receiving no satisfaction, calmly refilled, from a leather pouch, his pipe, which he had found on the mantel.

Elizabeth's thoughts began to take more distinct shape, and, in order to formulate them the more accurately, she spoke them aloud to the old man, finding it an assistance to have a hearer, though she supposed him unable to understand.

"Yet he wasn't a coward that evening he rode to attack the Hessians, — nor when he was wounded, — nor when he stood here waiting to be taken! He was no coward then, was he, Mr. Valentine?" Getting no answer, and irritated at the old man's owl-like immovability, she repeated, with vehemence, "Was he?"

Mr. Valentine had, by this time, begun to put things together in his mind.

"No. To be sure," he chirped, and then lighted his pipe with a small fagot from the fireplace, an operation that required a good deal of time.

Elizabeth now spoke more as if to herself. " Perhaps, after all, I may be wrong ! Yes, what a fool, to forget all the proofs of his courage ! What a blind imbecile, to think him afraid ! It must be that he acts from a delicate conception of honor. He would not encroach where another had the prior claim. He considers Colden in the matter. That's it, don't you think ? "

" Of course," said Valentine, blindly, not having paid attention to this last speech, and sitting down in his armchair.

" I can understand now," she went on. " He did not know of my engagement that time he made love, when his life was at stake."

" Then he's told you all about it ? " said the old man, beginning to take some interest, now that he had provided for his own comfort.

" About what ? " asked Elizabeth, showing a woman's consistency, in being surprised that he seemed to know what she had been addressing him about.

" About pretending he loved you, — to save his life," replied Mr. Valentine, innocently, considering that her supposed acquaintance with the whole secret made him free to discuss it with her.

Elizabeth's astonishment, unexpected as it was by him, surprised the old man in turn, and also gave

him something of a fright. So the two stared at
each other.

"Pretending he loved me!" she repeated, reflectively. "Pretending! To save his life! *Now I
see!*" The effect of the revelation on her almost
made Mr. Valentine jump out of his chair. "For
only *I* could save him!" she went on. "There was
no other way! Oh, *how* I have been fooled! I —
tricked by a miserable rebel! Made a laughing-
stock! Oh, to think he did not really love me, and
that I — Oh, I shall choke! Send some one to
me, — Molly, aunt Sally, any one! Go! Don't sit
there gazing at me like an owl! Go away and send
some one!"

Mr. Valentine, glad of reason for an honorable
retreat from this whirlwind that threatened soon to
fill the whole room, departed with as much activity
as he could command.

"Oh, what shall I do? What shall I do?"
Elizabeth asked of the air around her. "I must
repay him for his duplicity. I shall never rest a
moment till I do! What an easy dupe he must
think me! Oh – h – h!"

She brought her hand violently down on the
table but fortunately struck something compara-
tively soft. In her fury, she clutched this something, raised it from the table, and saw what it
was.

"*His* hat!" she cried, and made to throw it into the fire, but, with a woman's aim, sent it flying towards the door, which was at that instant opened by her aunt, who saved herself by dodging most undignifiedly.

"What is it, my dear?" asked Miss Sally, in a voice of mingled wonderment and fear.

"I'll pay him back, be sure of that!" replied Elizabeth, who was by this time a blazing-eyed, scarlet-faced embodiment of fury, and had thrown off all reserve.

"Pay whom back?" tremblingly inquired Miss Sally, with vague apprehensions for the safety of old Mr. Valentine, who had so recently left her niece.

"Your charming captain, your gentleman rebel, your gallant soldier, your admirable Peyton, hang him!" cried Elizabeth.

"*My* Peyton? I only wish he was!" sighed the aunt, surprised into the confession by Elizabeth's own outspokenness.

"You're welcome to him, when I've had my revenge on him! Oh, aunt Sally, to think of it! He doesn't love me! He only pretended, so that I would save his life! But he shall see! I'll deliver him up to the troops, after all!"

"Oh, no!" said Miss Sally, deprecatingly. Great as was the news conveyed to her by Elizabeth's speech, she comprehended it, and adjusted her mind to it, in an instant, her absence of outward demonstration being due to the very bigness of the revelation, to which any possible outside show of surprise would be inadequate and hence useless. Moreover, Elizabeth gave no time for manifestations.

"No," the girl went on. "You are right. He's able-bodied now, and might be a match for all the servants. Besides, 'twould come out why I shielded him, and I should be the laugh o' the town. Oh, *how* shall I pay him? How shall I make him *feel* —ah! I know! I'll give him six for half a dozen! I'll make *him* love *me*, and then I'll cast him off and laugh at him!"

She was suddenly as jubilant at having hit on the project as if she had already accomplished it.

"Make him love you?" repeated her aunt, dubiously. Her aunt had her own reasons for doubting the possibility of such an achievement.

"Perhaps you think I can't!" cried Elizabeth. "Wait and see! But, heavens! He's going away, —he won't come back, — perhaps he's gone! No, there's his hat!" She ran and picked it up from the corner of the doorway. "He won't go without his hat. He'll have to come here for it. He went to his room for his sword. He'll be here at any moment."

And she paced the floor, holding the hat in one hand, and lapsing to the level of ordinary femininity as far as to adjust her hair with the other.

"You'll have to make quick work of it, Elizabeth, dear," said the aunt, with gentle irony, "if he's going to-night."

"I know, I know, — but I can't do it looking like this." She laid the hat on the table, in order to employ both hands in the arrangement of her hair. "If I only had on my satin gown! By the lord Harry, I have a mind — I will! When he comes in here, keep him till I return. Keep him as if your life depended on it." She went quickly towards the door of the east hall.

"But, Elizabeth!" cried Miss Sally, appalled. "Wait! How —"

"How?" echoed Elizabeth, turning near the door. "By hook or crook! You must think of a way! I have other things on my mind. Only keep him till I come back. If you let him go, I'll never speak to you again! And not a word to him of what I've told you! I sha'n't be long."

"But what are you going to do?" asked the aunt, despairingly.

"Going to arm myself for conquest! To put on my war-paint!" And the girl hastened through the doorway, crossed the hall, called Molly, and ran upstairs to her room.

Miss Sally stood in the parlor, a prey to mingled feelings. She did not dare refuse the task thrown on her by her imperative niece. Not only her niece's anger would be incurred by the refusal, but also the niece's insinuations that the aunt was not sufficiently clever for the task. However difficult, the thing must be attempted. And, which made matters worse, even if the attempt should succeed, it would be a rewardless one to Miss Sally. If she might detain the captain for herself, the effort would be worth making. The aunt sighed deeply, shook her head distressfully, and then, reverting to a keen sense of Elizabeth's rage and ridicule in the event of failure, looked wildly around for some suggestion of means to hold the officer. Her eye alighted on the hat.

"He won't go without his hat, a night like this!" she thought. "I'll hide his hat."

She forthwith possessed herself of it, and explored the room for a hiding-place. She decided on one of the little narrow closets in either side of the doorway to the east hall, and started towards it, holding the hat at her right side. Before she had come within four feet of the chosen place, she heard the door from the south hall being thrown open, and, casting a swift glance over her left shoulder, saw the captain step across the threshold. She choked back her sensations, and gave inward thanks that the hat was hidden from his sight by herself. Peyton walked briskly towards the table.

Suddenly he stopped short, and turned his eyes from the table to Miss Sally, whose back was towards him.

" Ah, Miss Williams," said he, politely but hastily, " I left my hat here somewhere."

" Indeed ? " said Miss Sally, amazed at her own unconsciousness, while she tried to moderate the beating of her heart. At the same moment, she turned and faced him, bringing the hat around behind her so that it should remain unseen.

Peyton looked from her to the spinet, thence to the sofa, thence back to the table.

" Yes, on the table, I thought. Perhaps — " He broke off here, and went to look on the mantel.

Miss Sally, who had never thought the captain handsomer, and who smarted under the sense of being deterred, by her niece's purpose, from employing this opportunity to fascinate him on her own account, continued to turn so as to face him in his every change of place.

" I don't see it anywhere," she said, with childlike innocence.

Peyton searched the mantel, then looked at the chairs, and again brought his eyes to bear on Miss Sally. She blinked once or twice, but did not quail.

"'Tis strange!" he said. "I'm sure I left it in this room."

And he went again over all the ground he had already examined. Miss Sally utilized the times when his back was turned, in making a search of her own, the object of which was a safe place where she could quickly deposit the hat without attracting his attention.

Peyton was doubly annoyed at this enforced delay in his departure, since Elizabeth might come into the parlor at any time, and the meeting occur which he had, for a moment, hoped to avoid.

"Would you mind helping me look for it?" said he. "I'm in great haste to be gone. Do me the kindness, madam, will you not?"

"Why, yes, with pleasure," she answered, thinking bitterly how transported she would be, in other circumstances, at such an opportunity of showing her readiness to oblige him.

Her aid consisted in following him about, looking in each place where he had looked the moment before, and keeping the sought-for object close behind her.

Suddenly he turned about, with such swiftness that she almost came into collision with him.

"It must have fallen to the floor," said he.

"Why, yes, we never thought of looking there, did we?" And she followed him through another tour of the room, turning her averted head from side to side in pretendedly ranging the floor with her eyes.

"I know," he said, with the elation of a new conjecture. "It must be behind something!"

Miss Sally gasped, but in an instant recovered herself sufficiently to say:

"Of course. It surely *must* be — behind something."

Harry went and looked behind the spinet, then examined the small spaces between other objects and the wall. This search was longer than any he had made before, as some of the pieces of furniture had to be moved slightly out of position.

Miss Sally felt her proximity to the object of this search becoming unendurable. She therefore profited by Peyton's present occupation to conduct pretended endeavors towards the closet west of the fireplace. She noiselessly opened one of the narrow doors, quickly tossed the hat inside, closed the door, and turned with ineffable relief towards Peyton.

To her consternation she found him looking at her.

"What are you doing there?" he asked.

"Why, — looking in this closet," she stammered, guiltily.

"Oh, no, it couldn't be in there," said Peyton,

lightly. "But, yes. One of the servants migh have laid it on the shelf." And he made for th closet.

"Oh, no!"

Miss Sally stood against the closet doors and hel out her hands to ward him off.

"No harm to look," said he, passing around he and putting his hand on the door.

Miss Sally felt that, by remaining in the positioi of a physical obstacle to his opening the closet, sh would betray all. Acting on the inspiration of th instant, she ran to the centre of the room, an cried:

"Oh, come away! Come here!" and essayed ; well-meant, but feeble and abortive, scream.

"What's the matter?" asked Peyton, astonished.

"Oh, I'm going to faint!" she said, feignin; a sinkiness of the knees and a floppiness of th head.

"Oh, pray don't faint!" cried Peyton, running t(support her. "I haven't time. Let me call som(one. Let me help you to the sofa."

By this time he held her in his arms, and wa: thinking her another sort of burden than Ton Jones found Sophia, or Clarissa was to Rodericl Random.

The lady shrank with becoming and genuin(modesty from the contact, gently repelled him witl her hands, saying, "No, I'm better now, — but come," and took him by the arm to lead him further from the fatal closet.

But Peyton immediately released his arm.

"Ah, thank you for not fainting!" he said, with complete sincerity, and stalked directly back to the closet. Before she could think of a new device, he had opened the door, beheld the hat, and seized it in triumph. "By George, I was right! I bid you farewell, Miss Williams!" He very civilly saluted her with the hat, and turned towards the west door of the parlor.

Must, then, all her previous ingenuity be wasted? After having so far exerted herself, must she suffer the ignominious consequences of failure?

She ran to intercept him. Desperation gave her speed, and she reached the west door before he did. She closed it with a bang, and stood with her back against it. "No, no!" she cried. "You mustn't!"

"Mustn't what?" asked Peyton, surprised as much by her distracted eyes, panting nostrils, and heaving bosom, as by her act itself.

"Mustn't go out this way. Mustn't open this door," she answered, wildly.

He scrutinized her features, as if to test a sudden suspicion of madness. In a moment he threw off this conjecture as unlikely.

"But," said he, putting forth his hand to grasp the knob of the door.

"You mustn't, I say!" she cried. "I can't help it! Don't blame me for it! Don't ask me to explain, but you must not go out this way!"

She stood by her task now from a new motive, one that impelled more strongly than her fear of being reproached and derided by Elizabeth. Her own self-esteem was enlisted, and she was now determined not to incur her own reproach and derision. She perceived, too, with a sentimental woman's sense of the dramatic, that, though denied a drama of her own in which she might figure as heroine, here was, in another's drama, a scene entirely hers, and she was resolved to act it out with honor. Circumstances had not favored her with a romance, but here, in another's romance, was a chapter exclusively hers, a chapter, moreover, on whose proper termination the very continuation of the romance depended. So she would hold that door, at any cost.

Peyton regarded her for another moment of silence.

"Oh, well," said he, at last, "I can go the other way."

And, to her dismay, he strode towards the door of the east hall. She could not possibly outrun him thither. Her heart sank. The killing sense of failure benumbed her body.   He was already at the door, — was about to open it.   At that instant he stepped back into the parlor.   In through the doorway, that he was about to traverse, came Elizabeth.

CHAPTER XI.

MISS SALLY saw at a glance that her niece was dressed for conquest ; then, with immense relief and supreme exultation, but with a feeling of exhaustion, knowing that her work was done, she silently left the room by the door she had guarded, closed it noiselessly behind her, and went up-stairs to restore her worked-out energies.

Elizabeth wore a blue satin gown, the one evening dress she had, in the possibility of a candle-light visit from the officers at the outpost, brought with her from New York. Her bare forearms, and the white surface surrounding the base of her neck, were thus for the first time displayed to Peyton's view. A pair of slender gold bracelets on her wrists set off the smoothness of her rounded arms, but she wore no other jewelry. She had not had the time or the facilities to have her hair built high as a grenadier's cap, but she looked none the less commanding. She was, indeed, a radiant creature. Peyton, having never before seen her at her present advantage, opened wide his eyes and stared at her with a wonder whose openness was excused only by the suddenness of the dazzling apparition.

She cast on him a momentary look of perfect indifference, as she might on any one that stood in her way; then walked lightly to the spinet, giving him a barely noticeable wide berth in passing, as if he were something with which it was probably desirable not to come in contact. Her slight deviation from a direct line of progress, though made inoffensively, struck him like a blow, yet did not interrupt, for more than an instant, his admiration. He stood dumbly looking after her, at her smooth and graceful movement, which had no sound but the rustling of skirts, her footfalls being noiseless in the satin slippers she wore.

Peyton was not now as impatient as he had been to depart. In fact, he lost, in some measure, his sense of being in the act of departure. What he felt was an inclination to look longer on this so unexpected vision. She sat down at the spinet with her back towards him, and somehow conveyed in her attitude that she thought him no longer in the room. He felt a necessity for establishing the fact of his presence.

" Pardon me for addressing you," he said, with a diffidence new to him, taking up the first pretext that came to mind, " but I fear your aunt requires looking to.   She behaves strangely."

" Oh," said Elizabeth, lightly, too wise to give him the importance of pretending not to hear him, " she is subject to queer spells at times.   I thought you had gone."

She began to play the spinet, very quietly and unobtrusively, with an absence of resentment, and with a seemingly unconscious indifference, that gave him a paralyzing sense of nothingness.

Unpleasant as this feeling made his position, he felt the situation become one from which it would be extremely awkward to flee.   For the first time since certain boyhood fits of bashfulness, he now realized the aptness of that oft-read expression, " rooted to the spot."   That he should be thrown into this trance-like embarrassment, this powerlessness of motion, this feeling of a schoolboy first introduced to society, of a player caught by stage fright, was intolerable.

When she had touched the keys gently a few times, he shook off something of the spell that bound him, and moved to a spot whence he could get a view of her face in profile.   It had not an infinitesimal trace of the storm that had driven him from the room a short time before.   It was entirely serene.   There was on it no anger, no grief, no reproach of self or of another, no scorn.   There was pride, but only the pride it normally wore; reserve, but only the reserve habitual to a high-born girl in the presence of any but her familiars. It was hard to believe her the woman who had been stirred to such tremendous wrath a few minutes ago, by the disclosure that she had been deceived, her love tricked and misplaced. Rather, it was hard to believe that the scene of wrath had ever occurred, that this woman had ever been so stirred by such cause, that she had ever loved him, that he had ever dared pretend love to her. The deception and the confession, with all they had elicited from her, seemed parts of a dream, of some fancy he had had, some romance he had read.

As for Elizabeth, she knew not, thought not, whether, in bearing him hot resentment, she still loved him. She knew only that she craved revenge, and that the first step towards her desired end was to assume that indifference which so puzzled, interested, and confounded him. A weak or a stupid woman would have shown a sense of injury, with flashes of anger. An ordinarily clever woman would have affected disdain, would have sniffed and looked haughty, would have overdone her pretended contempt. It is true, Elizabeth had moved slightly out of her way to pass further from him, but she had done this with apparent thoughtlessness, as if the act were dictated by some inner sense of his belonging to an inferior race ; not with a visible intention of showing repulsion. It is true she had assumed ignorance of his presence, but she had given him to attribute this to a belief that he had left the room. When his voice declared his whereabouts, she treated him just as she would have treated any other indifferent person who was *not quite* her equal.

Peyton felt more and more uncomfortable. Would she continue playing the spinet forever, so perfectly at ease, so content not to look at him again, so assuming it for granted that, the operation of leave-taking being considered over between hostess and guest, the guest might properly be gone any moment without further attention on either side ?

He began to fear that, if he did not soon speak, his voice would be beyond recovery. So, with a desperate resolve to recover his self-possession at a single *coup*, he blurted out, bunglingly :

"'Tis the first time I have seen you in that gown, madam."

Elizabeth, not ceasing to let her fingers ramble with soft touch over the keyboard, replied, carelessly :

"I have not worn it in some time."

Having found that he retained the power of speech, he proceeded to utter frankly his latest thought, concealing the slight bitterness of it with a pretence of playful, make-believe reproach :

"'Tis not flattering to me, that you never wore it

while I was your guest, yet put it on the moment you thought I had departed."

She answered with good-humored lightness, "Why, sir, do you complain of not being flattered? I thought such complaints were made only by women, and only to their own hearts."

"If by flattery," said he, "you mean merited compliment, there are women who can never have occasion to complain of not receiving it."

"Indeed? When was that discovery made?"

"A minute ago, madam."

"Oh!" and she smiled with just such graciousness as a woman might show in accepting a compliment from a comparative stranger. "Thank you!"

"When I think of it," said he, "it seems strange that you — ah — never took pains to — eh — to appear at your best — nay, I should say, as your real self! — before me."

"Oh, you allude to my wearing this gown? Why, you must pardon my not having received you ceremoniously. *Your* visit began unexpectedly."

"Then somebody else is about to begin a visit that *is* expected?"

"Didn't you know? I thought all the house was aware Major Colden was to return in a week. He may be here to-night, though perhaps not till to-morrow."

"Confound that man!" This to himself, and

then, to her: "I was of the impression you did not love him."

"Why, what gave you that impression?"

"No matter. It seems I was wrong."

"Oh, I don't say that, — or that you're right, either."

"However," quoth he, with an inward sigh of resignation, "it is for *him* that you are dressed as you never were for me!"

She did not choose to ask what reason had existed for considering him in selecting her attire. It was better not to notice his presumption, and she became more absorbed in her music.

Peyton strode up and down a few moments, then sat by the table, and rested his cheek on his hand, wearing a somewhat injured look.

"Major Colden, eh?" he mused. "To think I should come upon him again!" He essayed to renew conversation. "I trust, Miss Philipse, when I am gone —" But Elizabeth was now oblivious of surroundings; the notes from the spinet became louder, and she began to hum the air in a low, agreeable voice. Peyton looked hopeless. Presently he stood up again, watching her.

Elizabeth brought the piece to a lively finish, rose capriciously, took up the flowers she had laid on the spinet earlier in the evening, put them in her corsage, and made to readjust the bracelet on her right arm. In this attempt, she accidentally dropped the bracelet to the floor. Peyton ran to pick it up. But she quickly recovered it before he could reach it, put it on, walked to the table and sat down by it, removed the flowers from her bosom to the table, took up the volume of "The School for Scandal," and turned the leaves over as if in quest of a certain page.

While she was looking at the book, Peyton took up the flowers. Elizabeth, as if thinking they were still where she had laid them, put out her hand to repossess them, keeping her eyes the while on the book. For a moment, her hand ranged the table in search, then she abandoned the attempt to regain them.

Peyton held them out to her.

"No, I thank you," she said, laying down the book, and went back to the spinet.

"Ah, you give them to me!" cried Peyton, with sudden pleasure.

"Not at all! I merely do not wish to have them now."

"Oh," said he, thinking to make account by finding offence where none was really expressed, "has my touch contaminated them for you?"

"How can you talk so absurdly?" And she resumed her seat at the spinet, and her playing.

Peyton stood holding the flowers, looking at her,

and presently heaved a deep sigh. This not moving her, he suddenly had an access of pride, brought himself together, and saying, with quick resolution, "I bid you good-night and good-by, madam," went rapidly towards the door of the east hall. But his resolution weakened when his hand touched the knob, and, to make pretext for further sight of her, he turned and went to go out the other door.

Elizabeth had had a moment of alarm at his first sign of departure, but had not betrayed the feeling. Now when, from her seat at the spinet, she saw him actually crossing the threshold near her, she called out, gently, "A moment, captain."

The pleased look on his face, as he turned towards her inquiringly, betrayed his gratification at being called back.

"You are taking my flowers away," she said, in explanation.

He plainly showed his disappointment. "Your pardon. My thoughtlessness. But you said you didn't wish to keep them." He laid them on the spinet.

"I do not, — yet a woman must allow very few hands to carry off flowers of her gathering."

She rose and took up the flowers and walked towards the fireplace.

"Then you at least take them back from my hands," said Peyton.

"Why, yes, — for this," and she tossed them into the fire.

He looked at them as they withered in the blaze, then said, "Have you any objection to my carrying away the ashes, Miss Philipse?"

She answered, considerately, "'Twill take you more time than you can lose, to gather them up."

"Oh, I am in no haste."

"Oh, then, I ask your pardon. A moment since, you were about to go."

"But now I prefer to stay."

"Indeed? May I ask the reason — but no matter."

But he felt that a reason ought to be forthcoming. "Why, you know, because — " And here he thought of one. "I wish to stay to meet Major Colden, of whom you say I am afraid. I shall prove to you at least I am no coward. After what you have said to me this night, I must in honor wait to face him."

"But it is late now. I don't think he will come till to-morrow."

"Then I can wait till to-morrow."

"But your duty calls you back to your own camp, now that your wound has healed."

"I think my wound has undergone a slight relapse. You shall see, at least, I am not afraid of your champion."

"If that is your only reason, — your desire to

quarrel with Major Colden,—I cannot invite you to remain."

"Well, then, to tell the truth, there *is* another reason. When I said, a while since, I had never seen you in that gown, I used too many words. I should have said I had never really seen you at all."

"Where were your eyes?" she asked, absently, seeming to take his words literally and to perceive no compliment.

"I was in a kind of waking sleep."

"It has been a time and place of hallucinations, I think. I, too, sir, have been, since I came here a week ago, under the strangest spell. A kind of light madness or witchery was over me, and made me act ridiculously, against my very will. A week ago, when you were disabled, I intended to give you up to the British, — as I should do now, if it would not be so troublesome — "

"'Twould be troublesome to *me*, I assure you," he said, interrupting.

"But at the last moment," she went on, "I did precisely the reverse of what I wished. Awhile ago, in this room, I seemed to be in the possession of some evil spirit, which made me say preposterous things. I can only remember some wild raving I indulged in, and some undeserved rudeness I displayed towards you. But, will you believe, the instant you left me, I recovered my right mind. I am like one returned from bedlam, cured, and you will pardon any incivility I may have done you in my peculiar state, I'm sure, since you speak of having been curiously afflicted yourself."

"Then you mean," he faltered, "you did not really love me?"

"Why, certainly I did not! How could you think I did? Something possessed my will. But, thank heaven, I am myself again. Why, sir, how could I? You know very little of me, sir, to think — Oh!" She covered her face with her hands. "What things must I have said and done, in my clouded state, to make you think that! You, — an enemy, a rebel, a person whose only possible interest to me arises from his enmity!"

Dazzled as he was by her newly discovered beauty, the imposition on him was complete. He saw this covetable being now indifferent to him, out of his power to possess, likely soon to pass into the possession of another.

"Pray try to forget awhile that enmity," he supplicated.

"I shall try, and then you can have no interest for me at all."

"Then don't try, I beg. I'd rather have an interest for you as an enemy than not at all."

"Why, really, sir — " She seemed half puzzled, half amused.

"Lord," quoth he, "how I have been deluded! I thought my love-making that night, feigned though it was, had wakened a response."

"Love-making, do you say? Will you believe me, sir, I don't remember what passed here that night, save the unaccountable ending, — my making you my guest instead of their prisoner."

"I wish you were pretending all this!"

"Why, if 'twould make you happier that I were, I wish so, too."

"How can you speak so lightly of such matters?"

"What matters?"

"Love, of course."

"Why, do men alone, because they laugh at women for taking love seriously, have the right to take it lightly? And of what love am I speaking lightly, — the love you say you feigned for me, or the love you say you thought you had awakened in me?"

"The love I vow I do *not* feign for you! The love I wish I *could* awaken in you!"

"Why, captain, what a change has come over you!"

"Yes. I have risen from my sleep. If you, in waking from yours, put off love, I, in waking from mine, took on love!"

She smiled, as with amusement. "A somewhat speedy taking on, I should say."

" Love's born of a glance, *I* say ! "

" Haven't I heard that before ? " reflectively.

" Aye, for I said it here when I did not mean it, and now I say it again when I do ! "

" And of what particular glance am I to suppose — "

" Of the first glance I cast on you when you entered this room in that gown. Yes, born of a glance — "

" Born of a gown, in that case, don't you mean ? " derisively.

" Of a gown, or a glance, or a what you wish."

" I don't wish it should be born at all."

" You don't wish I should love you ? "

" I don't wish you should love me or shouldn't love me. I don't wish you — anything. Why should I wish anything of one who is nothing to me ? "

" Nothing to you ! I would you were to me what I am to you ! "

" What is that, pray ? "

" An adorer ! "

" You are a — very amusing gentleman."

" You refuse me a glimpse of hope ? "

" You would like to have it as a trophy, I suppose. You men treasure the memories of your little conquests over foolish women, as an Indian treasures the scalps he takes."

"Lord! which sex, I wonder, has the busier scalping-knife?"

"I can't speak for all my sex. Some of us seek no scalps — "

"You don't have to. I make you a present of mine. I fling it at your feet."

"We seek no scalps, I say, — because we don't value them a finger-snap." And she gave a specimen of the kind of finger-snap she did not value them at.

"In heaven's name," he said, "say what you do value, that I may strive to become like it! What do you value, I implore you, tell me?"

"Oh,— my studies, for one thing, — my French and my music, — "

"Could I but translate myself into French, or set myself to an air!"

"Nay, I don't care for *comic* songs!"

"I see you like flowers. If I might die, and be buried in your garden, and grow up in the shape of a rose-bush — "

"Or a cabbage!"

"I fear you don't like that flower."

"Better come up in the form of your own Virginia tobacco."

"And be smoked by old Mr. Valentine? No, you don't like tobacco. Ah, Miss Philipse, this levity is far from the mood of my heart!"

"Why do you indulge in it, then?"

"I? Is it I who indulge in levity?"

"Assuredly, *I* do not!" Oh, woman's privilege of saying unabashedly the thing which is not!

"No," said he, "for there's no levity in the coldness with which beauty views the wounds it makes."

"I'm sure one is not compelled to offer oneself to its wounds."

"No, — nor the moth to seek the flame."

"La, now you are a moth, — a moment ago, a rosebush, —"

"And you are ten million roses, grown in the garden of heaven, and fashioned into one body there, by some celestial Praxiteles!"

"Dear me, am I all that?"

"Ay," he said, sadly, "and no more truly conscious of what it means to be all that, than any rose in any garden is conscious of what its beauty means!"

"Perhaps," she said, softly, feeling for a moment almost tenderness enough to abandon her purpose, "more conscious than you think!"

"Ah! Then you are not like common beauties, — as poor and dull within as they are rich and radiant without? You but pretend insensibility, to hide real feeling."

"I did not say so," she answered, lightly, bracing herself again to her resolution.

"But it is so, is it not?" he went on. "Your

heart and mind are as roseate and delicate as your face? You can understand my praises and my feelings? You can value such love as mine aright, and know 'tis worthy some repayment?"

But she was not again to be duped by low-spoken, fervid words, or by wistful, glowing eyes. She must be sure of him.

"I know, — I recall now," she said, with little apparent interest; "you spoke of love a week ago, with no less eloquence and ardor."

"More eloquence and ardor, I dare say, for then I did not feel love. Then my tongue was not tied by sense of a passion it could not hope to express one hundredth part of! And, even if my tongue had gift to tell my heart, I should not dare trust myself under the sway of my feelings. But I *do* love you now, — I do, — I do!"

"If now, why not before?"

"Haven't I said I've been blind to you until to-night? At first I regarded you as only an enemy to be turned to my use in my peril. Having been fortunate in that, I gave myself to other thoughts. But, thinking my false love had drawn true love from you, I saw I could not in honor leave you under a false belief. But now the falsehood has become truth. A week ago, I avowed a pretended passion, to gain my life! Now, I declare a real one, to gain your love!"

"What, you expect to take my love by storm, in reality, as you did, in appearance, a week ago?" She had risen from the music seat, and now stood with her back against the spinet, her hands behind her, her head turned slightly upward, facing him.

"I don't expect," said he. "I only hope."

"And what gives you reason to hope?"

"My own love for you. Love elicits love, they say."

"They say wrong, then. If that were true, there would be no unrequited lovers."

"Ay, but such love as mine, — how can it so fill me to overflowing, and not infect you?"

"Love is not an infectious disease. If it were, I should have no fear, — knowing myself love-proof."

"I can't believe that, — for a woman with no spark in herself could not light so fierce a flame in me, by the mere meeting of our eyes."

"If it should create in me such a disturbance as you seem to undergo, I shouldn't wish it to increase. But, I assure you, it isn't in me."

"Pray think it is. Only imagine it is there, and soon it will be."

She felt that the time was at hand to strike the blow.

"If I could be perfectly sure you spoke in earnest," she said, seeming to search his countenance for testimony.

" In earnest ! " he echoed.   " Great heavens, what evidence do you want ?   If there is an aspect of love I do not have, tell me, and I shall put it on."

" Yes, you are experienced in putting on the *aspects* of love."

" Oh, you well know I have no reason now for declaring a love I don't feel.   If you could be sure I spoke in earnest, you said, — what then ?   Tell me, and I shall find a way to convince you I *am* in earnest."

" Convince me first."

" ' Convince me,' you say.   And I say, ' Be convinced.'   By the Lord, never was so great a sceptic ! Is not your sense of your own charms sufficient to convince you of their effect ? "

" Mere words ! "

" I'll prove my love by acts, then ! "

" By what acts ? "

" By fighting for you or suffering for you, dying for you or living for you, as you may command."

" You can prove it thus.   Say, ' Long live the King ! ' "

He gazed at her a moment.   " No," he said.

" Say, ' Long live the King ! ' "   She went to the door, and paused on the threshold, looking at him, as if to give him a last opportunity.

" Long live the King — " he said.

She came back from the door.

"Of France!" he added.

"No," she cried, and dictated, "'Long live the King of Great Britain!'"

"Long live the King of Great Britain, — but not of America."

"No! 'Long live George the Third, King of Great Britain and the American colonies!'"

"Long live George the Third, King of Great Britain and — Ireland."

"'And of the American colonies.' Say it! Say it all!"

"Long live Elizabeth Philipse, queen of beauty in the United States of America!" he answered.

"You don't love me," said she, and set her mind to finding some other means by which he might evince what she knew he would never demonstrate in the way she had demanded. And she resolved his humiliation should be all the greater for the delay. "You don't love me."

"I do. I swear, on my knees."

"Then *get* on your knees!"

"I do!" He dropped on one knee.

"Both knees!"

"Both." He suited action to word.

"Bow lower."

"I touch the floor." He did so, with his forehead. "Are you convinced?"

"Yes." And she moved thoughtfully towards the door of the east hall.

"Ah! Convinced that I love you madly?" In obedience to a gesture, he remained on his knees.

"Perfectly convinced."

"Then, the reward of which you hinted?"

"Reward?"

"You said, if you could be sure I spoke in earnest. Now you admit you are sure. What then?"

She let her eyes rest on him a moment, without speaking, as he looked ardently and expectantly up at her from his kneeling attitude, while she took in breath, and then she flung her answer at him.

"What then? This! That you are now more contemptible and ridiculous and utterly non-existent, to me, than you have formerly been! That, whatever I may have done which seemed in your behalf, was partly from the strange insanity of which I have spoken, and partly from the most meaningless caprice! That, if you remain here till to-morrow, you may see me in the arms of the man I really love, and that he may not be as careless of the fate of a vagabond rebel as I am. And now, Captain Crayton, or Dayton, or Peyton, or whatever you please, of somebody or other's light horse, go or stay, as you choose; you're as welcome as any other casual passer-by, for all the comical figure your impudence has made you cut! Learn modesty, sir, and you may fare better in your next love-making, if you do not aim too high ! And that piece of advice is the reward I hinted at ! Good night ! "

And she whirled from the room, slamming behind her the mahogany door, at which Peyton stared for some seconds, in blank amazement, too overwhelmed to speak or move or breathe or think.

But gradually he came to life, slowly rose, stood for a moment thoughtful, fashioned his brows into a frown, drew his lips back hard, and muttered through his closed teeth :

" I'll stay and fight that man, at least ! "

And he sat down by the table, to wait.

CHAPTER XII.

THE CHALLENGE.

A VERY few moments had elapsed, and Peyton still sat by the table, in a dogged study, when the door from the south hall was opened slightly, and if he had looked he might have seen a pair of eyes peeping through the aperture. But he did not look, either then or when, some seconds later, the door opened wide and Miss Sally bobbed gracefully in.

It has been related how, after her brilliant but exhausting conduct of the important scene assigned her, she sought repose in her room. Looking out of her window presently, she saw something, of which she thought it advisable to inform Elizabeth. Therefore she came down-stairs. Did she listen at the door to the last part of that notable conversation? Ungallant thought, aroint thee! 'Tis well known women have little curiosity, and what little they have they would not, being of Miss Sally's station in life, descend to gratify by eavesdropping. Let it be assumed, therefore, that the much vaunted informant, feminine intuition, told Miss Sally of the end of the interview between her niece and the captain, both as to the time of that end and as to its nature.

She entered, tremulous with a vast idea that had blazed suddenly on her mind. Now that Elizabeth was quite through with Peyton, now that Peyton must be low in his self-esteem for Elizabeth's humiliation of him, and therefore likely to be grateful for consolatory attentions, Miss Sally might resume her own hopes. But there was no time to be lost.

"Your pardon, captain," she began, sweetly, with her most flattering smile. "I am looking for Miss Elizabeth."

"She was here awhile ago," replied Peyton, glumly, not bringing his eyes within range of the smile. "She went that way. I trust you've recovered from your attack."

"My attack?" inquiringly, with surprise.

"The queer spell, I think Miss Philipse called it. She said you were subject to them."

"Well, how does she dare —" She checked her tongue, lest she might betray the device for his detention. Something in his absent, careless way of associating her with a queer spell irritated her a little for the moment, and impelled her to retaliation. "I suppose that was not the only thing she said to you?" she added, ingenuously.

"No, — she said other things." He rose and

went to the fireplace, leaned against the mantel, and gazed pensively at the red embers.

"They don't seem to have left you very cheerful," ventured Miss Sally.

"Not so very damned cheerful!—I beg your pardon."

Miss Sally's moment of resentment had passed. Now was the time to strike for herself. She thought she had hit on a clever plan of getting around to the matter.

"Captain," said she, "you're a man of the world. I know it's presumptuous of me to ask it, but—if you would give me a word of advice—"

Peyton did not take his look from the fire, or his thoughts from their dismal absorption. He answered, half-unconsciously:

"Oh, certainly! Anything at all."

"You are aware, of course," she went on, with smirking, rosy confusion, "that Mr. Valentine is a widower."

"Indeed? Oh, yes, yes, I know."

"Yes, a widower twice over."

"How sad! He must feel twice the usual amount of grief."

"Why,—I don't know exactly about that."

"The poor man has my sympathy. Doubtless he is inconsolable." Peyton scarce knew what he was saying, or whom it was about.

"Why, no," said Miss Sally, averting her eyes, with a smiling shyness, "not altogether inconsolable. That's just it."

"Oh, is it?" said Peyton, obliviously.

"You may have noticed that he spends a good deal of time here at present," she went on.

"A good deal of time," he repeated. "There's doubtless some strong attraction."

"Yes. Perhaps I oughtn't to say it, but there *is* a strong attraction. In fact, he has proposed marriage to me, and now, as a man of the world to a woman of little experience, would you advise me to accept him?"

And she looked at the disconsolate officer so sweetly, it seemed impossible he should do aught but say it would be throwing herself away to bestow on an old man charms of which younger and warmer eyes were sensible. But he answered only:

"Certainly! An excellent match!"

For a time Miss Sally was speechless, yet open-mouthed. And then, for the length of one brief but fiery tirade, she showed herself to be her niece's aunt:

"Sir! The idea! I wouldn't have that old smoke-chimney if he were the last man on earth! I'd have given him his congé long ago, if it hadn't been that he might propose to my friend, the widow Babcock! I've only kept him on the string to prevent her getting him. When I want your advice,

Captain Peyton, I'll ask for it!   Excuse me, I must find Elizabeth.   I've news for her."

" News ? " he echoed, stupidly.

" Yes.   From my chamber window awhile ago I saw some one riding this way on the post-road, — Major Colden ! "

And she swept out by the same door that had closed, a few minutes before, on Elizabeth.

" Major Colden ! "   Peyton's teeth tightened, his eyes shot fire, his hand flew to his sword-hilt, as he spoke the name.

He went to the window, the same window at which Elizabeth had looked out a week ago, and peered through the panes at the night.

" Why, the ground is white," he said.   " It has begun to snow."

But, through the large flakes that fell thick and swiftly among the trees, he did not yet see any humankind approaching.   His view of the branch road was, at some places, obstructed by tall shrubbery that rose high above the palings and the hedge.

Yet through those flakes, assaulted by them in eyes and nostrils, invaded by them in ears and neck, humankind was riding.   It was, indeed, Colden that Miss Sally had seen through a fortuitous opening, which gave, between the trees, a view of the most eminent point of the post-road southward.   He was to conduct Elizabeth home the next day, but had availed himself of his opportunity to ride out to the manor-house that night, so as to have the few more hours in her society. He had this time taken an escort of two privates of his own regiment, but these men were not as well mounted as he, and, in his impatience, having seen the best their horses could do, and having passed King's Bridge, he had ridden ahead of them, leaving them to follow to the manor-house in their own speediest time. Thus it was that now he bore alone down from the post-road, his horse's feet making on the new-fallen snow no other sound than a soft crunching, scarce louder than its heavy breathing or its mouth-play on the bit, or the creak and clank of saddle, bridle, stirrups, pistols, and scabbard. His eyes dwelt eagerly on the manor-house, where awaited him light and warmth and wine, refuge from the pelting flakes, and, above all else, the joy-giving presence of Elizabeth. His breast expanded, he sighed already with relief; he approached the gate as a released soul, with admission ticket duly purchased by a death-bed repentance, might approach the gate of heaven.

But Peyton, looking out on the white world, saw no one. He did not change his attitude when the door reopened and Elizabeth and her aunt came into the parlor, arm in arm.

"You're sure 'twas he, aunt Sally?" Elizabeth had been saying.

"Positive. He should be here now," Miss Sally had replied.

Elizabeth cast a look of secret elation on the unheeding rebel captain, whose forehead was still against the window-pane. She saw a possible means of his still further degradation.

Suddenly he took a quick step back from the window, impulsively renewed his grasp of his sword hilt, and showed a face of resolute antagonism.

Elizabeth knew from this that he had seen Colden. She gave a smile of pleasant anticipation.

But Miss Sally had relapsed into her usual timid self. She held tightly to Elizabeth's arm.

"Oh, dear!" she whispered. "Won't something happen when those two meet?"

"I hope so!" said Elizabeth, placidly.

"Why?" demanded Miss Sally, beginning to weaken at the knees.

"If Colden sends him to the ground, in our presence, that will crown the fellow's humiliation."

Five brisk knocks, in quick succession, were heard from the outside door of the east hall.

Peyton walked across the parlor, turned, and stood facing the east hall door, the greater part of the room's length being between him and it. His hand remained on his sword. He paid no heed to Elizabeth, she paid none to him.

"His knock!" she said, and called out through

the east hall door: " 'Tis Major Colden, Sam. Show him here at once." She then stepped back from the door, to a place whence she could see both it and Peyton. Her aunt clung to her arm all the while, and now whispered, " Oh, Elizabeth, I fear there will be trouble!"

" If there is, it won't fall on your silly head," whispered Elizabeth, in reply.

From the hall came the sound of the drawing of bolts. Peyton did not take his eyes from the door.

A noise of footfalls, accompanied by clank of spurs and weapons, and in came Colden, his hat in his left hand, snow on his hat and shoulders, his cloak open, his sword and pistols visible, his right hand ungloved to clasp Elizabeth's.

She received him with such a cordial smile as he had never before had from her.

" Elizabeth!" he cried, — beheld only her, hastened to her, took her proffered hand, bent his head and kissed the fingers, raised his eyes with a grateful, joyous smile, — and saw Peyton standing motionless at the other side of the room. The smile vanished; a look of amazement and hatred came.

" I wish you a very good evening, *Major* Colden!"

Peyton said this in a voice as hard and ironical as might have come from a brass statue.

For the next few seconds the two men stood

gazing at each other, the women gazing at the men.
At last the Tory major found speech :

" Elizabeth, — what does it mean ? Why is this
man here, — again ? "

" 'Tis rather a long story, Jack, and you shall hear
it all in time," said Elizabeth, determined he should
never hear the true story.

Before she could continue, Colden suffered a start
of alarm to possess him, and asked, quickly :

" Are any of his troops here ? "

" No ; he is quite alone," she answered.

Colden at once took on height, arrogance, and
formidableness.

" Then why have not your servants made him
a prisoner ? " he asked.

" Why," said she, " you being mentioned to-night,
in his presence, he made some kind of boast of not
fearing you, and I, divining how soon you would be
here, thought fit his freedom with your name should
best be paid for at *your* hands, major."

" Ay, major," put in Peyton, " and I have stayed
to receive payment ! "

Colden thought for a short while. Then he said,
" A moment, Elizabeth. Your pardon, Miss Williams," and drew Elizabeth aside, and spoke to her
in a low tone : " We have only to temporize with
him. Two of my men have attended me from my
quarters. I had a better horse, and rode ahead, in

my eagerness to see you. My two fellows will be here soon, and the business will be done."

But such doing of the business did not suit Elizabeth's purpose. "I wish to humiliate the man," she answered Colden, inaudibly to the others; "to take down his upstart pride! 'Twould be no shame to him, to be made prisoner by numbers."

"What, then?" asked Colden, dubiously.

"Bring down the coxcomb, before us women, in an even match!"

To prevent objections, she then abruptly went from Colden, and resumed her place at her aunt's side.

Colden stood frowning, not half pleased at her hint. It occurred to him, as it did not to her, that the mere allegiance and favoring wishes of herself were not sufficient possessions to ensure victory in such a match as she meant. Elizabeth, accustomed to success, did not conceive it possible that the chosen agent of her own designs could fail. But the chosen agent had, in this case, wider powers of conception.

All this time, Captain Peyton had stood as motionless as a figure in a painting. He now interrupted Colden's meditations with the gentle reminder:

"I am waiting for my payment, Major Colden."

Colden was not a man of much originality. So,

in his instinctive endeavor to gain time, he bungled out the conventional reply, "You wish to seek a quarrel with me, sir?"

"Seek a quarrel?" retorted Peyton. "Is not the quarrel here? Has not Miss Philipse spoken of an offence to your name, for which I ought to receive payment from you? Gad, she'd not have to speak twice to make *me* draw!"

Colden continued to be as conventional as a virtuous hero of a novel. "I do not fight in the presence of ladies, sir," said he.

"Nor I," said Peyton. "Choose your own place, in the garden yonder. With snow on the ground, there's light enough."

And Harry went quickly, almost to the door, near which he stopped to give Colden precedence.

"Nay," put in Elizabeth, "we ladies can bear the sight of a sword-cut or two. Wait for us," and she would have gone to send for wraps, but that Colden raised his hand in token of refusal, saying:

"Nay, Elizabeth. I will not consent."

"Come, sir," said Peyton. "'Tis no use to oppose a lady's whim. But if you make haste, we may have it over before they can arrive on the ground."

In handling his sword-hilt, Peyton had pulled the weapon a few inches out of the scabbard, and now, though he did not intend to draw while in the house, he unconsciously brought out the full length of what remained of the blade. For the time he had forgotten the sword was broken, and now he was reminded of it with some inward irritation.

Meanwhile Colden was answering :

" There's no regularity in such a meeting. Where are the seconds ? "

" I'll be your second, major," cried Elizabeth. " Aunt Sally, second Captain Peyton."

" Ridiculous ! " said the major.

" Anything to bring you out," said Peyton, as desirous of avenging himself on Elizabeth, through her affianced, as she was to complete her own revenge through the same instrument. " I'll fight you with half a sword. I'd forgotten 'tis all I've left."

" I would not take an advantage," said the New Yorker.

" Then break your own sword, and make us equal," said the Virginian.

" I value my weapon too much for that."

Peyton smiled ironically. But he tried again.

" Then I shall be less scrupulous," said he. " I *will* take an advantage. The greater honor to you, if you defeat me. You take the broken sword, and lend me yours."

He held out his hilt for exchange.

Colden pretended to laugh, saying :

"Am I a fool to put it in your power to murder me?"

"*I'll* tell you what, gentlemen," put in Elizabeth. "Use the swords above the chimney-place, yonder. They are equal."

"Yes!" cried Peyton.

But Colden said:

"I will not so degrade myself as to cross swords, except on the battle-field, with one who is a rebel, a deserter, and no gentleman."

Peyton turned to Elizabeth with a smile.

"Then you see, madam," said he, "'tis no fault of mine if my affronts go unpunished, since this gentleman must keep his courage for the battle-field! Egad," he added, sacrificing truth for the sake of the taunt, "you Tories need all the courage there you can save up in a long time! I take my leave of this house!"

He thrust his sword back into the scabbard, bowed rapidly and low, with a flourish of his hat, and went out by the same door Elizabeth had used in her own moment of triumph. He unbolted the outside door himself, before black Sam could come from the settle to serve him. Snowflakes rushed in at the open door. He plunged into them, swinging the door close after him. Out through the little portico he went, down the walk outside the very parlor window through which he had looked out awhile ago,

"'I TAKE MY LEAVE OF THIS HOUSE!'"

but through which he did not now look in as he passed; through the gate, and up the branch road to the highway. He was possessed by a confusion of thoughts and feelings, — temporary and superficial elation at having put Elizabeth's preferred lover in so bad a light, wild ideas of some future crossing of her path, swift dreams of a future conquest of her in spite of all, a fierce desire for such action as would lead to that end. He was eager to rejoin the army now, to participate in the fighting that would bring about the humbling of her cause and make it the more in his power to master her. He heeded little the snow that impeded his steps as his boots sank into it, and which, in falling, blinded his eyes, tickled his face, and clung to his hair. The tumult of flakes was akin to that of his feelings, and he was in mood for encountering such opposition as the storm made to his progress.

Arriving at the post-road, he turned and went northward. At his left lay the great lawn fronting the manor-house, and separated from the road by hedge and palings. He could see, across the snowy expanse, between the dark trunks and whitened branches of the trees, the long front of the manor-house, its roof and its porticoes already covered with snow, the light glowing in the one exposed window of the east parlor. As he quieted down within, he felt pleasantly towards the house, to which his week's half-solitary residence in it, with the comfort he had enjoyed there and the books he had read, had given him an attachment. He cast on it a last affection-ate look, then breasted the weather onward, wonder-ing what things the future might have in store for him.

He had little fear of not reaching the American lines in safety. It was unlikely that any of the ene-my's marauders would be out on such a night, and more unlikely that any regular military movement would be making on the neutral ground. He ex-pected to meet no one on the road, but he would keep a sharp lookout in all directions as he went, and, in case of any human apparition, would take to the fields or the woods. But all the world, thought he, would stay within doors this white night.

Sliding back a part of every step he took in the snow, he passed the boundary of the Philipse lawn, and that of such part of the grounds as included, with other appurtenances, the garden north of the house. He had come, at last, to a place where the fence at his left ended and the forest began. He had, a moment before, cast a long look backward to assure himself the road was empty behind him. He now trudged on, his eyes fixed ahead.

From behind a low pine-tree, at the end of the fence, two dark figures glided up to the captain's rear, their steps noiseless in the snow. One of them caught both his forearms at the same instant, and pulled them back together, as with grips of iron. A second pair of hands placed a noose about his wrists, and quickly tightened it. Ere he could turn, his first assailant released the bound arms to the second, drew a pistol, and thrust the muzzle close to Peyton's cheek, whereupon the second man said :

" Your pardon, captain.   Come quietly, or you're a dead man ! "

CHAPTER XIII.

THE UNEXPECTED.

PEYTON'S somewhat elate exit from the parlor was followed by a moment of silence and inertia on the part of the three who remained there. But Elizabeth's chagrin was speedily translated into anger against Major Colden.

"Why didn't you fight him?" she demanded of that gentleman, who was flinching inwardly, but who maintained a pale and haughty exterior.

"What was the use?" he replied. "He's reserved for the gallows. If my two men were here! Why not send your servants after him? Sam is a powerful fellow, and Williams is shrewd and strong."

Elizabeth ignored Colden's reply, and answered her own question, thus:

"It was because you remembered the time he disarmed you, three years ago."

"You may think so, if you choose," he replied, in the patient manner of one who quietly endures unjust reproaches when self-defence is useless.

"You will find refreshments in the dining-room," said Elizabeth, coldly. "Sam will show you to your room."

"I would rather remain with you," he replied.

"I would rather be alone with my aunt a while."

A deep sigh expressed his dejecting sense of how futile it would be to oppose her.

"As you will," he then said, and, bowing gravely, left the parlor.

Elizabeth's feelings now burst out.

"Oh," she exclaimed to her aunt, "what a chicken-hearted copy of a man! And he calls himself a soldier! I wonder where he found the spirit to volunteer!"

"From you, my dear," replied Miss Sally. "Didn't you urge him to take a commission?"

"And that rebel fellow had the best of it all through," Elizabeth went on. "I was to see him laid low by his rival, as my crowning revenge! How he swaggered out! with what a look of triumph in his eye! And — aunt Sally! He won't come back! I shall never see him again!"

"Why, child, do you wish to?""

"Of course not! But I can't have him go away with the laugh on his side! He made me ridiculous after my trying to stab him with my love for the other man. *Such* another man! Oh, the rebel must come back!"

"But he isn't likely to," said Miss Sally.

"Oh, what shall I do?" wailed the niece.

"Elizabeth, I'll wager you're still in love with him!"

"I'm not! I hate him!—Well, what if I am? He loved me, I'm sure, the last time he said it. But, good heavens, he's going farther away every instant!"

She clasped her hands, and, for once, looked at her aunt for help, like a distressed child on the verge of weeping.

"Why don't you call him back?" said Miss Sally.

"I? Not if I die for want of seeing him!—I know! I *will* send the servants after him." And she started for the door, but stopped at her aunt's comment:

"But that will be as bad as calling him yourself."

"Not at all, you empty pate!" cried Elizabeth, who had become, in a moment, all action. "While he's going around by the road, Williams and Sam shall cut across the garden, lie in wait, and take him by surprise. He has no weapon but a broken sword, and they can make him prisoner. They shall bring him back here bound, and he'll think he's to be turned over to the British after all!"

"But what then?"

"Why, he shall be left alone here, well guarded, for

half an hour, and then I'll happen in, give him an opportunity to make love again, and I can yield gracefully! Don't you see?"

"Then you *do* love him?" said the aunt.

"I don't know. However, I don't love Jack Colden. Not a word to him, of this! I'm going to give orders to the men."

As she entered the hall, she met Colden, who was coming from the dining-room with Mr. Valentine. The major had limited his refreshments to two glasses of brandy and water, swallowed in quick succession. Mr. Valentine, who was smoking his pipe, held Colden fraternally by the arm.

"What, Elizabeth, are you still angry?" said Colden, stopping as she passed.

"Excuse me, I have something to see to," said the girl, coolly, hurrying away from him.

He made a slight movement to follow her, but old Valentine drew him into the parlor, saying :

"Come, major, you'll see the lady enough after she's married to you. I was just going to say, the last lot of tobacco I got — "

"Oh, damn your tobacco!" said the other, jerking his arm from the old man's tremulous grasp.

"Damn my tobacco?" echoed Mr. Valentine, quite stupefied.

"Yes. I've matters more important on my mind just now."

"The deuce!" cried the old man. "What could be more important than tobacco?"

And he stood looking into the fire, muttering to himself between furious puffs.

Colden sought comfort of Miss Sally. "Was ever a woman as unreasonable as Elizabeth?" he said to her. "She'd have had me lower myself to meet that rebel vagabond as one gentleman meets another."

But Miss Sally was not going to betray her own disappointment by showing a change from her oft-expressed opinion of the rebel captain, — particularly in the presence of Mr. Valentine. So she answered:

"You met him so once, three years ago."

"I had a less scrupulous sense of propriety then," replied Colden, raging inwardly.

"But, as he's a rebel and deserter," pursued Miss Sally, "was it not your duty as a soldier to take him, just now?"

"I'd have done so, had my men been here," growled the major. "Elizabeth ought to've had her servants hold him. I had half a mind to order them, in the King's name, but I never can bring myself to oppose her, she's so masterful! By George, though, I'll have him yet! My two fellows will soon come up. They shall give chase. He will leave tracks in the snow."

Colden went to the window, and peered out as

Peyton himself had done not long before. The flakes were coming down as thick as ever.

"I don't see my rascals yet!" he muttered. "They've stopped at the tavern, I'll warrant."

And he continued to gaze eagerly out, impatient that his men should arrive before the new-fallen snow should cover his enemy's tracks.

Old Mr. Valentine, having exhausted his present stock of mutterings, now walked over to Miss Sally, who had sat down near the spinet.

"Miss Williams," said he, "this is the first chance I've had to speak to you alone in a week."

"But we're not alone," said Miss Sally, motioning her head towards Colden.

"He's nobody," contemptuously replied the octogenarian. "A man that damns tobacco is nobody. So you may go ahead and speak out. What's your answer, ma'am?"

"Oh, Mr. Valentine, not now! You must give me time."

"That's what you said before," he complained.

She had, indeed, said it before, scores of times.

"Well, give me more time, then," she replied.

"How much?" asked the old man, in a matter-of-fact way.

"Oh, I don't know! Long enough for me to make up my mind."

Thus far, this conversation had followed in the

exact lines of many that had preceded it, but now Mr. Valentine made a departure from the customary form.

"I think," said he, "if my other two wives had taken as long as you to make up their minds, I shouldn't have been twice a widower by now."

"Oh, Mr. Valentine!" said Miss Sally, in a sweetly reproachful way. "Now you know — "

But he cut her speech off short. "Very likely," said he. "I don't know. Well, take your time. Only please remember I haven't so very much time left! Better take me while I'm here to be had! Good night, ma'am!" And he went to the dining-room to fortify himself for his long homeward walk through the snow.

In crossing the hall, he saw Cuff on the settle in Sam's place. In the dining-room he met Molly, who was clearing the table of the supper that Colden had disdained. He asked her the whereabouts of Williams, and she replied that the steward and Sam had gone out on some order of Miss Elizabeth's. Deciding to await Williams's return, the old man sat down before the dining-room fire, and was soon peacefully snoring.

Elizabeth had gone up-stairs to watch from her darkened window the issue of the expedition of Williams and Sam, who had gone out by the kitchen, equipped respectively with rope and pistol. While they were in the immediate vicinity of the house, she could not see them from her elevation, but presently she beheld them glide swiftly across a white open space in the garden, cross a stile, and disappear among the trees and bushes between the garden and the post-road. Turning her eyes to the road itself, that lonely highway now called Broadway,[9] she made out a solitary figure toiling forward through the whirling whiteness, — and she gave a sigh, the deepest and longest with which her frame had ever trembled.

Meanwhile Miss Sally remained in the parlor, thinking it best not to go to Elizabeth unless sent for ; while Colden continued to stand at the window, showing his impatience for the arrival of his two soldiers in a tense contracting of the brow, in a restless shifting from foot to foot, and in intermittent stifled curses.

As he kept his eyes on the place where the branch road left the highway, he did not see that part of the lawn walk which led from the garden. But suddenly a slight noise drew his look towards the portico before the east hall.

"Who are these coming?" he cried, startling Miss Sally out of her musings and her chair.

"Are they your men?" she asked, hastening to join him at the window.

"No, mine are mounted," said he. "Why, —

these are Williams and Sam, — and they are bringing, — yes, it is he! They're bringing him back a prisoner! She has done it, after all, without consulting me!" And he strode to the centre of the room, in the utmost elation.

Miss Sally weakened at the imminent prospect of a meeting between the two enemies in the changed circumstances, and felt the need of her niece's support.

"I must tell Elizabeth they have him," she said, and ran out to the east hall, and thence to the dining-room, just in time to avoid seeing Peyton led in through the outer door, which Cuff had opened at Williams's call.

The steward and Sam conducted their prisoner immediately into the parlor. There Colden stood, with a rancorously jubilant smile, to receive him.

Peyton's wrists were as Williams had tied them. He was without his hat, which had been knocked off in a brief struggle he had essayed against his captors in a moment when Sam had lowered the pistol. There was a little fresh snow on his hair, and more on his shoulders. The feet of his boots were cased with it. His left arm was held by Williams, who carried the broken sword, having taken it from the scabbard at the first opportunity. Peyton's other arm was grasped by the huge, bony left hand of Sam, who held the cocked pistol in his right. The two men walked with him to the centre of the parlor, and stopped.

"By George," said he, turning his face towards Sam, with fire in his eyes, "had the snow not killed the sound of your sneaking footsteps till you'd caught my arms behind, I'd have done for the two of you!"

"Good, Williams!" said Colden. "Place him on that chair, and leave him here with me. But stay in the hall on guard."

"So Miss Elizabeth ordered us, sir," said Williams, dryly, and, with Sam, conducted Peyton to the chair, on which he sat willingly.

"Of course she did," replied Colden. "Was it not at my suggestion?"

Peyton looked sharply up at the major, who regarded him with the undisguised pleasure of hate about to be satisfied.

Williams handed the broken sword to Colden, saying, "This was the only weapon he had, sir. We grabbed him before he could use it. We ran out behind him from the roadside, and he couldn't hear us for the snow."

"Ay, or the pair of you couldn't have taken me!" said Peyton, with hot scorn and defiant gameness.

Colden, with the piece of sword, motioned Williams to go from the room.

"Leave the door ajar a little," he added, "so you can hear if I call."

Peyton uttered a short laugh of derision at this piece of prudence. The steward and Sam withdrew to the hall, where Sam remained, while Williams went in search of Elizabeth for further orders. As soon as she had assured herself, by watching and listening, that Peyton was safe in the parlor, she had stolen quietly down-stairs to the dining-room, where she had met her aunt, with whom the steward now found her sitting. She told him to get the duck-gun, make sure it was loaded and primed, and to wait with Sam on the settle in the hall. She then requested her aunt to remain in the dining-room, silently returned to the hall, and took station by the door leading from the parlor, — the door which Williams, at Colden's command, had left slightly ajar. Her original plan, she felt, might have to be altered by reason of Colden's having obtruded his hand into the game, a possibility she had not, in roughly sketching that plan, taken into account. It was in order to have the guidance of circumstance, that she now put herself in the way of hearing, unseen, what might pass between the two men. Meanwhile, through the snow-storm, Colden's two soldiers, who had indeed tarried at the tavern for the heating up of their interiors, were blasphemously urging their sleepy horses towards the manor-house.

In the parlor, the two enemies were facing each

other, Peyton on his chair, his tied wrists behind him, Colden standing at some distance from him, holding the broken sword. As soon as they were alone, Peyton uttered another one-syllabled laugh, and said:

"The hospitality of this house beats my recollection. One is always coming back to it."

"You'll not come back the next time you leave it!" said Major Colden, his eyes glittering with gratified rancor.

"And when shall that time be?" asked Peyton, airily.

"As soon as two of my men arrive, whom I outrode on my way hither to-night. They attended me out of New York. I shall be generous and give them over to you, to attend you *into* New York."

"Thanks for the escort!"

"'Tis the only kind you rebels ever have, when you enter New York," sneered the major.

"We shall enter it with an escort of our own choosing some day! And a sorry day that for you Tories and refugees, my dear gentleman!"

"But if that day ever comes, *you'll* have been rotting underground a long time,—and thanks to *me*, don't forget that!"

"Thanks to *her*, you coward!" cried Peyton. "'Twas she that sent her servants after me! You didn't dare try taking me, alone!"

"Bah!" said Colden, hotly, "I might have pistolled you here to-night" — and he placed his hand on the fire-arm in his belt — "but for the presence of the ladies!"

"Was it the ladies' presence," retorted Peyton, contemptuously, "or the fact that you're a devilish bad shot?"

Neither man heard the door moved farther open, or saw Elizabeth step through the aperture to the inner side of the threshold, where she stopped and watched. Peyton's back was towards her, and Colden's rage at the last words was too intense to permit his eyes to rove from its object.

"Damn you!" cried the major. "I'd show you how bad a shot I am, but that I'd rather wait and see you on the gallows!"

"Will *she* come to see me there, I wonder?" said Peyton, half thoughtfully. "She ought to, for it's her work sends me there, not yours! 'Twill not be *your* revenge when they string me up, my jolly friend!"

Taunted beyond all self-control, the Tory yelled:

"Not mine, eh? Then I'll have mine now, you dog!"

With that, he strode forward and struck Harry a fierce blow across the face with the flat side of Harry's own broken sword.

Harry merely blinked his eyes, and did not flinch.

He turned pale, then red, and in a moment, first clearing his voice of a slight huskiness, said, quietly :

"That blow I charge against you both, — the lady as well as you!"

Colden had stepped back some distance after delivering the blow. Something in Harry's answer seemed to infuriate still further the devil awakened in the Tory's body, for he cried out :

"The lady as well as me, — yes! And this, too!"

And he advanced on Peyton, to strike a second time.

"Stop! How dare you?"

The cry was Elizabeth's. It startled Colden so that he loosened his hold of the broken sword before he could deliver the blow. At that instant, she caught his arm in her one hand, the sword-guard in her other. She tore the weapon from his grasp, and faced him with a countenance as furious as his own.

"What do you mean?" he cried.

For answer she struck him in the face with the flat of the sword, as he had struck Peyton. "You sneak!" she said.

He recoiled, and stood staring, a ghastly image of bewilderment and consternation. After a moment he turned livid.

"Ah! I see now!" he gasped. "You love him!"

"Yes!" came the answer, prompt and decided.

He gazed at her with such an expression as a

painter of hell might put into the face of a lost soul, and he said, faintly, in a kind of articulate moan :

"I might have known!"

Suddenly there came from the outer night the exclamation, quick and distinct :

"Whoa!"

CHAPTER XIV.

THE BROKEN SWORD.

THE sound wrought a transformation in Colden. His face lighted up with malevolent joy.

"You love too late!" he cried, to Elizabeth. "My men are there! They shall take him to New York a prisoner, at last!"

"But not delivered up by me, thank God!" replied Elizabeth, while Peyton rose quickly from his chair, and Colden reeled like a drunken man to the window.

She went behind Peyton, and, with the edge of the broken sword, hacked rather than cut through one of the outer windings that bound his wrists together, whereupon she speedily uncoiled the rope.

"You were my prisoner. I set you free!" she said, dropped the rope to the floor, and handed him the broken sword.

He took the weapon in his right hand, and imprisoned Elizabeth with his left arm.

"I'm more your prisoner now than ever!" he said. "You've cut these bonds. Will you put others on me?"

"Sometime, — if we can save your life!" she answered.

Both turned their eyes towards Colden.

The Tory officer had drawn his sword, and was motioning, in great excitement, to his soldiers outside.

"This way, men!" he shouted. "To the front door! Damn the louts! Can't they understand?" He beat upon the window with his sword, knocking out panes of glass. "Come through that door, I say! Quick, curse you, there's a prisoner here, with a price for his taking! Ay, that's it! Some one in the hall there, open the front door to my men!"

The sound now came of knocks bestowed on the outside door, and of Sam's heavy tread on the hall floor.

"Williams! Sam!" shouted Elizabeth. "Don't let them in!"

The heavy tread was heard to stop short. The knocking on the outer door was resumed.

"Let them in, I say," roared Colden, too proud to go himself to the door. "I command it, in the name of the King!"

"Obey your mistress," cried Peyton, to those in the hall. "I command it, in the name of Congress!"

Colden was silent for a moment, then suddenly threw open the window and called out, "This way, men! Quick!"

And he drew pistol, and stood ready with steel

and ball to guard the window by which his men were to enter. A new, wild ferocity was on his face, a new, nervous hardness in his body, as if the latent resolution and strength which a prudent man keeps for a great contest, on which his all may depend, were at last aroused. In such a mood, the man who, governed by interest, may have seemed a coward all his life becomes for the once supremely formidable. At last he thinks the stake worth the play, at last the prize is worth the risk, and because it is so he will play and risk to the end, hazarding all, not yielding while he breathes. Having opened the theme which alone, of all themes, shall transform his irresolution into action, he will, Hamlet like, "fight upon this theme until" his "eyelids will no longer wag." So was Colden aroused, transfigured, as he stood doubly armed by the window, waiting for his men to clamber in.

"What shall we do, dear?" said Elizabeth.

"Fight!" replied Peyton, tightening at the same time his right palm around his broken sword, and his left around the hand she had let him take, — for she had moved from the embrace of his arm.

"Ay, there are only two of them," she said, as two burly forms appeared in the open window, one behind the other.

"There will be three of us, you'll find!" cried Colden. "This time I'll take a hand, if need be."

"You must not stay here," said Peyton to Elizabeth, quickly. "Things will be flying loose in a moment!"

"I won't leave you!" said she.

"Go! I beg you, go!" he said, releasing her hand, and stepping back.

Meanwhile, Colden's men bounded in through the window. Rough, sturdy fellows were they, who landed heavily on the parlor floor, and blinked at the light, drawing the while the breeches of their short muskets from beneath their coats. Their hats and shoulders were coated with snow.

"Take that rebel alive, if you can!" ordered Colden. "He's meant to hang! Stun him with your musket-butts!"

The men quickly reversed their weapons, and strode heavily towards Harry. To their surprise, before they could bring down their muskets, which required both hands of each to hold, Harry dashed forward between them, thinking to cut down Colden with his broken sword, possess himself of the latter's pistol, shoot one of the soldiers, and meet the other on less unequal terms. He saw a possibility of his leaping through the open window and fleeing on one of the soldiers' horses, but the idea was accompanied by the thought that Elizabeth might be made to suffer for his escape. Her safety now depended on his getting the mastery over his three would-be captors. So, ere the two astonished fellows could turn, Harry had leaped within sword's reach of his doubly armed enemy.

But Colden was now as alert as rigid, and he opposed his officer's sword against Peyton's broken cavalry blade, guarding himself with unexpected swiftness, and giving back, for Harry's sweeping stroke, a thrust which only the quickest and most dexterous movement turned aside from entering the Virginian's lungs. As Harry stepped back for an instant out of his adversary's reach, the Tory raised his pistol. At the same moment the two soldiers, having turned about, rushed on Peyton from behind. He heard them coming, and half turned to face them. Their movement had for him one fortunate circumstance. It kept Colden from shooting, for his bullet might have struck one of his own men.

Now Elizabeth had not been idle. At the moment when Harry had stepped back from her and bade her go, she had run to the door of the east hall, and called Williams and Sam. While Peyton had been engaging Colden near the window, the steward and the negro had entered the parlor, and she had excitedly ordered them to Peyton's aid. Williams still had the duck-gun, Sam the pistol. Thus it occurred that, as Peyton half turned from Colden towards the two soldiers, these last-named saw Williams and Sam rush in between them and their prey. Before Williams could bring his duck-gun to bear, he was struck down senseless by one of the musket blows first intended for Peyton. Another blow, and from another musket, had been aimed at Sam's woolly head, but the negro had put up his left hand and caught the descending weapon, and at the same time had discharged his pistol at the weapon's holder. But Williams, in falling, had knocked against the darky, and so disturbed his aim, and the ball flew wide. The man who had brought down Williams now struck Sam a terrible blow with the musket-club, on the temple, and the negro dropped like a felled ox.

During this brief passage, Peyton had returned to close quarters with Colden. The latter, who had lowered his pistol when his men had last approached Peyton, and who had resumed the contest of swords unequal in size and kind, now raised the pistol a second time. But it was caught by the hands of Elizabeth, who had run around to his left, and who now, suddenly endowed with the strength of a tigress, wrenched it from him as she had wrenched the broken sword earlier in the evening. She tried to discharge the pistol at one of the two soldiers, as they, relieved of the brief interposition of Williams and Sam, were again taking position to bring down their muskets on Peyton's head while he continued at sword-work with Colden. But the pistol snapped without going off, whereupon Elizabeth hurled it in the face of the man at whom she had aimed. The blow disconcerted him so that his musket fell wide of Peyton, who at the same instant, having seen from the corner of his eye how he was menaced, leaped backward from under the other descending musket. Then, taking advantage of the moment when the muskets were down, he ran to the music seat before the spinet, and mounted upon it, thinking rightly that the infuriated major would follow him, and that he might the better execute a certain manœuvre from the vantage of height. Colden indeed rushed after him, and thrust at him, Peyton sweeping the thrusts aside with pendulum-like swings of his own short weapon. His thought was to send the point that menaced him so astray that he might leap forward and cleave his enemy with a downward stroke before the Tory could recover his guard. But Colden pressed him so speedily that he was at last fain to step up from the music seat to the spinet, landing first on the keyboard, which sent out a frightened discord as he alighted on it. Finding the keys an uncertain footing, he took another step, and stood on the body of the instrument, so that Colden would be at the disadvantage of thrusting upwards. But Colden, seeming to tire a little after a few such thrusts, called to his men:

"Shoot the dog in the legs!"

Both men aimed at once. Elizabeth screamed. Peyton leaped down from his height to the little space behind the spinet projection, where he had hidden a week before. Here he found himself well placed, for here he could be approached on one side only,—unless his adversaries should follow his example and come at him from the top of the spinet.

Colden attacked him with sword, at the open side, and shouted to his men :

"One of you get on the spinet. The other crawl under. We have him now."

Still guarding himself from his enemy's thrusts, Peyton heard one of the men leap from the music seat to the spinet, and the other advance creeping, doubtless with gun before him, under the instrument. Peyton sank to his knees, placed his shoulder under the back edge of the spinet's projection, and, warding off a downward movement of Colden's sword, turned the instrument over on its side, checking the creeping man under it, and throwing the other fellow to the floor some feet away. As the spinet fell, one of its legs, rising swiftly into the air, knocked Colden's blade upward, and the Tory leaped back lest Peyton might avail himself of the opening. But the spinet-leg itself hindered Peyton from doing so. Colden rushed forward again, thrusting as he did so. Peyton leaped aside, made a swift half-turn, and landed a stroke on Colden's sword-hand, making the Tory cry out and drop the sword. Harry put his foot on it and cried:

"You're at my mercy! Beg quarter!"

But the man who had been thrown from the top of the spinet now returned to the attack, coming around that end of the upset instrument which was opposite the end where Colden had menaced Harry. Seeing this new adversary, Harry retreated past Colden, in order to put himself in position. The soldier hastened after him, with upraised musket. At this moment, Peyton saw himself confronted by Elizabeth, who pulled open the door of the south hall. He stopped short to avoid running against her.

"Save yourself!" she cried, and pushed him through the open doorway, flinging the door shut upon him, a movement which the pursuing soldier, stayed for a moment by collision with Colden, was not in time to prevent. Harry heard the key move in the lock, and knew that Elizabeth had turned it, and that he was safe in the south hall, with a minute of vantage which he might employ as he would.

Elizabeth withdrew the key from the locked door, just as the pursuing soldier arrived at that door. The man, in his excitement, violently tried to open the door. Colden, who was wrapping a handkerchief around his wounded hand, shouted to the man:

"You fool, she has the key! Take it from her!"

"You shall kill me first!" she cried, and ran from the man towards the open window, stepping over the prostrate bodies of Sam and Williams as she went.

"After her! She'll throw it into the snow!" cried Colden.

This much Harry heard through the door, and heard also the heavy tread of the soldier's feet in pursuit of the girl. His mind imaged forth a momentary picture of the fellow's rough hands laid on the delicate arms of Elizabeth, of her body clasped by the man in a struggle, her white skin reddened by his grasp. The spectacle, imaginary and lasting but an instant, maddened Peyton beyond endurance, made him a giant, a Hercules. He threw himself against the door repeatedly, plied foot and body in heavy blows. Meanwhile Elizabeth had reached the window, and thrown the key far out on the snow-heaped lawn. She had no sooner done so than the man laid his clutch on her arm.

"Fly, Peyton, for God's sake! For my sake!" she shouted.

"You shall pay for aiding the enemy, if he does!" cried Colden. "Don't let her escape, Thompson!"

At that instant the locked door gave way, and in burst Harry, having broken, to save Elizabeth from a rude contact, the barrier she had closed to save his life. That life, which he had once saved by callously assailing her heart, he now risked, that her body might not suffer the touch of an ungentle hand. So swift and sudden was his entrance, that he had crossed the room, and floored Elizabeth's captor, with a deep gash down the side of the head, ere Colden made a step towards him.

The man who had been under the fallen spinet had now extricated himself, and regained his feet, and he and Colden rushed on Peyton at once. Elated by having so speedily wrought Elizabeth's release, and reduced the number of his able adversaries to two, Peyton bethought himself of a new plan. He fled through the deep doorway to the east hall, and took position on the staircase. He turned just in time to parry Colden's sword, which the major had picked up and made shift to hold in his wrapped-up, wounded hand. Harry saw that an opportune stroke might send the sword from his enemy's numb and weakening grasp, and his heart swelled with anticipated triumph, until he heard Colden's hoarse cry:

"Shoot him, James, while I keep him occupied!"

This order was now the more practicable from Harry's being on the stairs, above Colden, a great part of his body exposed to an aim that could not endanger his antagonist. Breathing heavily, his eyes afire with hatred, Colden repeated his attacks, while Harry saw the other's musket raised, the barrel looking him in the eyes. He leaped a step higher, swung his broken sword against the pendent chandelier, knocked the only burning candle from its socket, and threw the hall into darkness. A moment later the gun went off, giving an instant's red flame, a loud crack, and a smell of gunpowder smoke. Harry heard a swift singing near his right ear, and knew that he was untouched.

Lest Colden's sword, thrust at random, might find him in the dark, Harry instantly bestrode the stair-rail, and dropped, outside the balustrade, to the floor of the hall. He grasped his half-sword in both hands, so as to put his whole weight behind it, and made a lunge in the direction of a muttered curse. The curse gave way to a roar of pain and rage, and Colden's second follower dropped, spurting blood in the darkness, his shoulder gashed horribly by the blunt end of Peyton's imperfect weapon. Harry now ran back to the parlor, to deal with Colden in the light, the latter's greater length of weapon giving a greater searching-power in the darkness. In the parlor Elizabeth stood waiting in suspense. Sam was sitting on the floor and staring stupidly at Williams, who was now awake and rubbing his head, and the Tory first fallen was still senseless. Harry had no sooner taken this scene in at a glance, than Colden was upon him.

The major's eyes seemed to stand out like blazing carbuncles from the face of some deity of rage.

"G—d d—n your soul!" he screamed, and thrust. The point went straight, and Elizabeth, seeing it protrude through the back of Harry's coat, near the left side of his body, uttered a low cry, and sank half-fainting to her knees. Colden shouted with triumphant laughter. "Die, you dog! And when you burn in hell, remember I sent you there!"

But the evil joy suddenly faded out of Colden's face, for Harry Peyton, smiling, took a forward step, grasped near the hilt the sword that seemed to be sheathed in his own body, forced it from Colden's hand, and then drew it slowly from its lodgment. No blood discolored it, and none oozed from Harry's body.

The Virginian's quick movement to escape the thrust had left only a part of his loose-fitting coat exposed, and Colden's sword had passed through it, leaving him unhurt. Colden's momentary appearance of victory had been the means of actual defeat.

The Tory major saw his cup of revenge dashed from his lips, saw himself deprived of sword and sweetheart, neither chance left of living nor motive left for life. His rage collapsed; his hate burst like a bubble.

"Kill me," he said, quietly, to Peyton.

His look, innocent of any thought to draw compassion, quite disarmed Harry, who stood for a moment with moistening eyes and a kind of welling-up at the throat, then said, in a rather unsteady voice :

"No, sir! God knows I've taken enough from you," and he looked at Elizabeth, who had risen and was standing near him. Softened by the triumphant outcome for her love, she, too, was suddenly sensible of the defeated man's unhappiness, and her eyes applauded and thanked Harry.

"You've taken what I never had," said Colden, with a chastened kind of bitterness, "yet without which the life you give me back is worthless."

"Make it worth something with this," and Peyton held Colden's sword out to him.

"What! You will trust me with it?" said Colden, amazed and incredulous, taking the sword, but holding it limply.

"Certainly, sir!"

Colden was motionless a moment, then placed his arm high against the doorway, and buried his face against his arm, to hide the outlet of what various emotions were set loose by his enemy's display of pity and trust.

Harry gently drew Elizabeth to him and kissed her. Yielding, she placed her arms around his neck, and held him for a moment in an embrace of her own offering. Then she withdrew from his clasp, and when Colden again faced them she had resumed that invisible veil which no man, not even the beloved, might pass through till she bade him.

"You will find me worthy of your trust, sir," said Colden, brokenly, yet with a mixture of manly humility and honorable pride.[10]

"I am so sure of that," said Harry, "that I confide to your care for a time what is dearest to me in the world. I ask you to accompany Miss Philipse to her home in New York, when it may suit her convenience, and to see that she suffer nothing for what has occurred here this night."

"You are a generous enemy, sir," said Colden, his eyes moistening again. "One man in ten thousand would have done me the honor, the kindness, of that request!"

"Why," said Harry, taking his enemy's hand, as if in token of farewell, "whatever be the ways of the knaves, respectable and otherwise, who are so cautious against tricks like their own, thank God it's not so rotten a world that a gentleman may not trust a gentleman, when he is sure he has found one!"

Turning to Elizabeth, he said: "I beg you will leave this house at dawn, if you can. Williams and Sam, there, will be little the worse for their knocks, and can look after the fellows on the floor."

"And you," she replied, "must go at once. You must not further risk your life by a moment's waiting.　Cuff shall saddle Cato for you.　I sha'n't rest till I feel that you are far on your way."

He approached as if again to kiss her, but she held out her hand to stay him.　He took the hand, bent over it, pressed it to his lips.

"But, —" he said, in a tone as low as a whisper, "when —"

"When the war is over," she answered, softly, "let Cato bring you back."

NOTES

NOTES.

Note 1. (Page 41.)

"The old county historian." Rev. Robert Bolton,
born 1814, died 1877. His "History of the County of
Westchester," especially the revised edition published
in 1881, is a rich mine of "material." Among other
works that have served the author of this narrative in
a study of the period and place are Allison's "History
of Yonkers," Cole's "History of Yonkers," Edsall's "History of Kingsbridge," Dawson's "Westchester County
during the Revolution," Jones's "New York during the
Revolution," Watson's "Annals of New York in the
Olden Time," General Heath's "Memoirs," Thatcher's
"Memoirs," Simcoe's "Military Journal," Dunlap's "History of New York," and Mrs. Ellet's "Domestic History
of the Revolution." For an excellent description of the
border warfare on the "neutral ground," the reader should
go to Irving's delightful "Chronicle of Wolfert's Roost."
Cooper's novel, "The Spy," deals accurately with that subject, which is touched upon also in that good old standby,
Lossing's "Pictorial Field-book of the Revolution." Phil-

ipse Manor-house has been carefully written of by Judge Atkins in a Yonkers newspaper, and less accurately by Mrs. Lamb in her "History of New York City," and Marian Harland in "Some Colonial Homesteads and Their Stories." Of general histories, Irving's "Life of Washington" treats most fully of things around New York during the British occupation, and these things are interestingly dealt with in local histories, such as the "History of Queens County," Stiles's "History of Brooklyn," Barber and Howe's "New Jersey Historical Collections," etc., as well as in such special works as "Onderdonk's "Revolutionary Incidents."

NOTE 2. (Page 47.)

Of Colonel Gist's escape, Bolton gives the following account: "The house was occupied by the handsome and accomplished widow of the Rev. Luke Babcock, and Miss Sarah Williams, a sister of Mrs. Frederick Philipse. To the former lady Colonel Gist was devotedly attached; consequently, when an opportunity afforded, he gladly moved his command into that vicinity. On the night preceding the attack, he had stationed his camp at the foot of Boar Hill, for the better purpose of paying a special visit to this lady. It is said that whilst engaged in urging his suit the enemy were quietly surrounding his quarters; he had barely received his final dismissal from Mrs. Babcock when he was startled by the firing of musketry. . . . It appears that all the roads and bridges had been well guarded by the enemy, except the one now called Warner's Bridge, and that Captain John Odell upon the first alarm led off his troops through the woods on the west side of the Saw Mill [River]. Here Colonel Gist joined them. In the meantime Mrs. Babcock, having stationed herself in one of the dormer windows of the parsonage, aided their escape whenever they appeared, by the waving of a white handkerchief."

The British attack was under Lieutenant-Colonel Simcoe, whose journal shows that his force so far outnumbered Gist's that the latter's only sensible course was in flight. About the year 1840, trees cut down near the site of Gist's camp were found to contain balls buried six inches in the wood.

Note 3. (Page 76.)

The three generals arrived on the *Cerberus*, May 25th. All the histories say that they arrived " with reinforcements." It is true, troops were constantly arriving at Boston about that time, but none came immediately with the three generals. The *Connecticut Gazette* (published in New London) printed, early in June, this piece of news, brought by a gentleman who had been in Boston, May 28th : " Generals Burgoyne, Clinton, and Howe arrived at Boston last Friday in a man-of-war. No troops came with them. They brought over 25 horses." It is a wonder that Frothingham, in his admirably complete history of the siege of Boston, missed even this little circumstance. Probably everybody has read the incident thus related by Irving : " As the ships entered the harbor and

the rebel camp was pointed out, Burgoyne could not restrain a burst of surprise and scorn. 'What!' cried he;
'ten thousand peasants keep five thousand King's troops
shut up! Well, let us get in and we'll soon find elbow
room!'" I don't think Irving relates anywhere the se-
quel, which is that when, after his surrender, Burgoyne
marched with his conquered army into Cambridge. an old
woman shouted from a window to the crowd of spectators,
"Give him elbow room!" This story ought to be true, if
it is not.

NOTE 4.   (Page 89.)

It was in a letter under date of October 4. 1778, that
Washington wrote: "What officer can bear the weight of
prices that every necessary article is now got to? A rat
in the shape of a horse is not to be bought for less than
£200 : a saddle under thirty or forty."

NOTE 5.   (Page 124.)

Captain Cunningham was the British provost marshal,
as everybody knows, whose name became a synonym for
wanton cruelty in the treatment of war prisoners. He
had come to New York before the Revolution, and had
kept a riding school there. As soon as the war broke out
he took the royal side. It was he who had in charge the
summary execution of Nathan Hale. He would often
amuse himself by striking his prisoners with his keys and
by kicking over the baskets of food or vessels of soup
brought for them by charitable women, who, he said,
were the worst rebels in New York. He died miserably

in England after the war. His career is briefly outlined in Sabine's "Loyalists." As to the manner in which Peyton, if caught, would have died, it must be remembered that in the American Revolution the rope served in many a case which, occurring in Europe or in one of our later wars, would have been disposed of with the bullet. Writing of General Charles Lee, John Fiske says : "There is no doubt that Sir William Howe looked upon him as a deserter, and was more than half inclined to hang him without ceremony." Then, as now, a deserter in time of war was liable to death if caught at any subsequent time, his case being worse than that of a spy, who was liable to death only if caught before getting back to his own lines. There was, by the way, much unceremonious hanging on the "neutral ground." Not far from the Van Cortlandt mansion there still stood, in Bolton's time, "a celebrated white oak, in the midst of a pretty glade, called the Cowboy Oak," from the fact that many of the Tory raiders had been suspended from its branches during the war of Revolution.

Note 6. (Page 127.)

I am not sure whether the saying, "The corpse of an enemy smells sweet," attributed to Charles IX. of France, in allusion to Coligny, is historical or was the invention of a romancer. It occurs in Dumas's "La Reine Margot."

Note 7. (Page 136.)

Mr. Valentine's unwillingness to lend aid was doubtless due to the frequency of such incidents as one that had occurred to his neighbor, Peter Post, in 1776. Post's estate occupied the site of the present town of Hastings. He gave information to Colonel Sheldon regarding the movements of some Hessians, and afterwards deceived the Hessians as to the whereabouts of Sheldon's own cavalry. Thereby, Sheldon's troop was enabled to surprise the Hessians, and defeat them in a short and bloody conflict. The Hessians' comrades later caught Post, stripped him, beat him to insensibility, and left him for dead. He recovered of his injuries. His house, a small stone one, became a tavern after the Revolution, and was a celebrated resort of cock-fighters and hard-drinkers. Not far north of Hastings is Dobbs Ferry, which was occupied by both armies alternately, during the Revolution. Further north is Sunnyside, Irving's house, elaborated from the original Wolfert's Roost, and beyond that are Tarrytown, where André was stopped and taken in charge, and Sleepy Hollow. Enchanted ground, all this, hallowed by history, legend, and romance.

Note 8. (Page 179.)

The secret passage or passages of Philipse Manor-house have not been neglected by writers of fiction, history, and magazine articles. The passage does not now exist, but there are numerous traces of it. The different writers do not agree in locating it. The author of an interesting story for children, " A Loyal Little Maid," has it that the passage was reached through an opening in the panelling of the dining-room, this opening concealed by a tall clock. I think Marian Harland says that a closet in one of the parlors or chambers connects with the secret passage. Both these assumptions are wrong. Mr. R. P. Getty has pointed out in the northwestern corner of the cellar what seems to have once been the entrance to the passage. One authority quotes a belief "that from the cellar there was a passage to a well now covered by Woodworth Avenue," and that this was to afford access to what may have been a storage vault. A man who was born in 1821 says that, when a boy, he saw, near the house, a dry cistern, from the bottom of which was an arched passage towards the Hudson, large enough for a man six feet tall to pass through. Judge Atkins says that the well was opposite the kitchen door, and had, at its western side, about ten feet deep, a chamber in which butter was kept. One writer locates an ice-house where Judge Atkins places this well, and says a subterranean arched way led northward as far as the present Wells Avenue. "The ice-house was formerly, it is said, a powder-magazine." Many years ago, the coachman of Judge Woodworth used to say he had "gone through an underground passage all the way from the manor-house to the Hudson River." Judge Atkins has written interesting legends of the manor-house, involving the secret passage and other features.

NOTE 9. (Page 259.)

"That lonely highway now called Broadway." A block of houses and another street now lie between that highway and the east front of the manor-house. The building is closely hemmed in by the sordid signs of progress. Ugly houses, in crowded blocks, cover all the great surrounding space that once was thick forest, fair orchards, gardens, fields, and pastoral rivulet. The Neperan or Saw Mill River flows, sluggish and scummy, under streets and houses. A visit to the manor-house, now, would spoil rather than improve one's impression of what the place looked like in the old days. Yet the house itself remains well preserved, for which all honor to the town of Yonkers. There is in our spacious America so much room for the present and the future, that a little ought to be kept for the past. It is well to be reminded, by a landmark here and there, of our brave youth as a people. A posterity, sure to value these landmarks more than this money-grabbing age does, will reproach us with the destruction we have already wrought. Worse still than the crime of obliterating all human-made relics of the past, is the vandalism of nature herself where nature is exceptionally beautiful. To rob millions of beauty-lovers, yet to live, of the Palisades of the Hudson, would bring upon us the amazement and execration of future centuries. This earth is an entailed estate, that each generation is in honor bound to hand down, undefaced, undiminished, to its successor. In order that a close-clutched wallet or two may wax a little fatter, shall we bring upon ourselves a cry of shame that would ring with increasing bitterness through the ages, — shall we invite the execration merited by such greed as could so outrage our fair earth, such stolid apathy as could stand by and see it done? Shall an alien or two, as hard of soul as the stone in which he traffics, mar the Hudson that Washington patrolled, rob countless eyes, yet unopened, of a joy; countless minds, yet to waken, of an inspiration; countless hearts, yet to beat, of a thrill of pride in the soil of their inheriting? Shall some future reader wonder why Irving, deeming it "an invaluable advantage to be born and brought up in the neighborhood of some grand and noble object in nature," should have thanked God he was born on the banks of the Hudson? I write this with the sound of the blowing up of Indian Head still echoing in my ears, and knowing nothing done by Government to protect the next fair Hudson headland from similar destruction.

NOTE 10. (Page 281.)

It is probable that Colden served with his brigade when it fought in the South in the last part of the war. He was afterwards lost at sea, leaving no heir. He was of a family prominent in New York affairs, both before the Revolution and afterwards, and which was intermarried with other New York families of equal prominence, as may be seen in the "New York Genealogical and Biographical Record," the "New England Genealogical and Historical Register," and similar publications. It is probable that Sabine means this Colden when he mentions a Captain Colden, of the First Battalion of New Jersey Volunteers. That he was a major, however, is certain, from the official British Army lists published in Hugh

Gaines's " Universal Register " for the years of the Revolution.

People curious about Harry Peyton's military record may consult Saffel's " Lists of American Officers," Heitman's " Manual," and a large work on " Virginia Genealogies," by H. E. Hayden, published at Wilkesbarre. To the reader who demands a happy ending, it need be no shock to learn that Peyton, having risen to the rank of major, was killed at Charleston, S. C., May 12, 1780. For a love story, it is a happy ending that occurs at the moment when the conquest and the submission are mutual, complete, and demonstrated. A love to be perfect, to have its sweetness unembittered, ought not to be subjected to the wear and tear of prolonged fellowship. So subjected, it may deepen and gain ultimate strength, but it will·lose its intoxicating novelty, and become associated with pain as well as with pleasure. We may be sure that the love of Peyton and Elizabeth was to Harry a sweetener of life on many a night encampment, many a hard ride, in the campaign of 1779, and in the spring of 1780, and exalted him the better to meet his death on that day when Charleston fell to the British; and that to Elizabeth, while it receded into further memory, it kept its full beauty during the half century she lived faithful to it. Her sisters were married into the English nobility, gentry, and military, but Elizabeth died in Bath, England, in March, 1828, unmarried. Colonel Philipse had moved with his family to England when the British quitted New York in 1783. Many other Tories did likewise. Some went to England, but more to Canada, the greater part of which was then a wilderness. Many of the Tory officers got commissions in the English army.

No Tory family did more for the King's cause in America, lost more, or got more in redress, than the De Lancey family, which had been foremost in the administration of royal government in the province of New York. It had great holdings of property in New York City, elsewhere on the island of Manhattan, and in various parts of Westchester County, notably in Westchester Township, where De Lancey's mills and a fine country mansion were a famous landmark " where gentle Bronx clear winding flows." The founder of the American family was a French Huguenot of noble descent. The family was represented in the British army and navy before the Revolution. One member of it, a young officer in the navy, at the breaking out of the war, resigned his commission rather than serve against the Colonies, but most of the other De Lancey men were differently minded. Oliver De Lancey, a member of the provincial council, was made a brigadier-general in the royal service, and raised three battalions of loyalists, known as " De Lancey's Battalions." Of these battalions, the Tory historian, Judge Jones, says : " Two served in Georgia and the Carolinas from the time the British army landed in Georgia until the final evacuation of Charleston. One of these, during this period, was commanded by Lieutenant-Colonel Stephen De Lancey, the other by Colonel John Harris Cruger. The third battalion, during the whole war, was employed solely in protecting the wood-cutters upon Lloyd's Neck,

Queens County, L. I. This General De Lancey's son, Oliver De Lancey, Junior, was educated in Europe, took service with the 17th Light Dragoons, was a captain when the Revolution began, a major in 1778, a lieutenant-colonel in 1781, and, on the death of Major André, adjutant-general of the British army in America. Returning to England, he became deputy adjutant-general of England; as a major-general, he was also colonel of the 17th Light Dragoons; was subsequently barrack-master general of the British Empire, lieutenant-general, and finally general. When he died he was nearly at the head of the English army list. This branch of the family became extinct when Sir William Heathcoate De Lancey, the quartermaster-general of Wellington's army, was killed at Waterloo.

The James De Lancey who commanded the Westchester Light Horse was a nephew of the senior General Oliver De Lancey, and a cousin of the Major Colden of this narrative. His troop was not "a battalion in the brigade of his uncle," Bolton's statement that it was so being incorrect; its operations were limited to Westchester County. It raided and fought for the King untiringly, until it was almost entirely killed off, at the end of the war, by the persistent efforts of our troops to extirpate it.

The members of this corps were called "Cowboys" because, in their duty of procuring supplies for the British army, they made free with the farmers' cattle. Like the other conspicuous Tories, this James De Lancey was attainted by the new State Government, and his property was confiscated. Local historians draw an effective picture of him departing alone from his estate by the Bronx, turning for a last look, from the back of his horse, at the fair mansion and broad lands that were to be his no more, and riding away with a heavy heart. He went, with many shipfuls of Tory emigrants, to Nova Scotia, and became a member of the council of that colony. His uncle went to England and died at his country house, Beverly, Yorkshire, in 1785. I allude to the case of this family, because it was typical of that of a great many families. The Tories of the American Revolution constitute a subject that has yet to be made much of. They were the progenitors of English-speaking Canada.

The act of attainder that deprived the De Lanceys of their estates, deprived Colonel Philipse of his. It was passed by the New York legislature, October 22, 1779. The persons declared guilty of "adherence to the enemies of the State" were attainted, their estates real and personal confiscated, and themselves proscribed, the second section of the act declaring that "each and every one of them who shall at any time hereafter be found in any part of this State, shall be, and are hereby, adjudged and declared guilty of felony, and shall suffer death as in cases of felony, without benefit of clergy." Acts of similar import were passed in other States. Under this act, Philipse Manor-house was forfeited to the State about a year after the time of our narrative. The commissioners whose duty it was to dispose of confiscated property sold the house and mills, in 1785, to Cornelius P. Lowe. It underwent several transfers, but little change, becoming at length the property of Lemuel Wells, who held it a long time and, dying in 1842, left it to his nephew. The town of Yonkers grew up around it, and on May 1, 1868, purchased it for municipal use. The fewest possible alterations were made in it. These are mainly in the north wing, the part added by the second lord of the manor in 1745. On the first floor, the partition between dining-room and kitchen was removed, and the whole space made into a court-room. On the second floor, the space formerly divided into five bed-rooms was transformed into a council-chamber, the garret floor overhead being removed. The new city hall of Yonkers leaves the old manor-house less necessary for public purposes. May the old parlors, where the besilked and bepowdered gentry of the province used to dance the minuet before the change of things, not be given over to baser uses than they have already served.

Allusion has been made, in different chapters of this narrative, to the Hessians who daily patrolled the roads in the vicinity of the manor-house. This duty often fell to Pruschank's yagers, the troop to which belonged Captain Rowe, whose love story is thus told by Bolton: "Captain Rowe appears to have been in the habit of making a daily tour from Kingsbridge, round by Miles Square. He was on his last tour of military duty, having already resigned his commission for the purpose of marrying the accomplished Elizabeth Fowler, of Harlem, when, passing with a company of light dragoons, he was suddenly fired upon by three Americans of the water guard of Captain Pray's company, who had ambuscaded themselves in the cedars. The captain fell from his horse, mortally wounded. The yagers instantly made prisoners of the undisciplined water guards, and a messenger was immediately despatched to Mrs. Babcock, then living below, in the parsonage, for a vehicle to remove the wounded officer. The use of her gig and horse was soon obtained, and a neighbor, Anthony Archer, pressed to drive. In this they conveyed the dying man to Colonel Van Cortlandt's. They appear to have taken the route of Tippett's Valley, as the party stopped at Frederick Post's to obtain a drink of water. In the meantime an express had been forwarded to Miss Fowler, his affianced bride, to hasten without delay to the side of her dying lover. On her arrival, accompanied by her mother, the expiring soldier had just strength enough left to articulate a few words, when he sank exhausted with the effort." The room in which he died is in the well-known mansion in Van Cortlandt Park.

The incident of the horse, related in an early chapter, has a likeness to an adventure that befell one Thomas Leggett early in the Revolutionary war. He lived with his father on a farm near Morrisania, then in Westchester County, and was proud in the possession of a fine young mare. A party of British refugees took this animal, with other property. They had gone two miles with it, when, from behind a stone wall which they were passing, two Continental soldiers rose and fired at them. The man with the mare was shot dead. The animal immediately turned round and ran home, followed by the owner, who had dogged her captors at a distance in the hope of recovering her.